Critical Acclaim For
Ross Thomas
and
YELLOW-DOG CONTRACT

more . . .

Also by Ross Thomas

VOODOO, LTD.
TWILIGHT AT MAC'S PLACE
THE FOURTH DURANGO
OUT ON THE RIM
BRIARPATCH
MISSIONARY STEW
THE MORDIDA MAN
THE EIGHTH DWARF
CHINAMAN'S CHANCE
YELLOW-DOG CONTRACT
THE MONEY HARVEST
IF YOU CAN'T BE GOOD
THE PORKCHOPPERS
THE BACKUP MEN
THE FOOLS IN TOWN ARE ON OUR SIDE
THE SINGAPORE WINK
CAST A YELLOW SHADOW
THE COLD WAR SWAP

Under the pseudonym Oliver Bleeck
NO QUESTIONS ASKED
THE HIGHBINDERS
THE PROCANE CHRONICLE
PROTOCOL FOR A KIDNAPPING
THE BRASS GO-BETWEEN

ROSS THOMAS

YELLOW-DOG CONTRACT

THE MYSTERIOUS PRESS

Published by Warner Books

A Time Warner Company

MYSTERIOUS PRESS EDITION

Copyright © 1977 by Ross E. Thomas, Inc.
All rights reserved.

Cover Design and Illustration by Peter Thorpe

This Mysterious Press Edition is published by arrangement with the author.

The Mysterious Press name and logo are trademarks of Warner Books, Inc.

 Mysterious Press books are published by
Warner Books, Inc.
   1271 Avenue of the Americas
   New York, NY 10020

 A Time Warner Company

Printed in the United States of America

First Mysterious Press Printing; November, 1993

10 9 8 7 6 5 4 3 2 1

for
John and Mary Lou Burwell
with thanks
for the loan of the farm

1

The Proper Villain slowed them down. I heard the car when it turned in and I could tell it was going far too fast, but I didn't look around because I was up in the tree fixing the swing. The tree was the huge old cottonwood, probably fifty feet high, that grew on the other side of the house next to the pond.

The swing was a long single length of three-quarter-inch manila rope and to its other end I had already wired a gunnysack stuffed with rags and an old army blanket. The idea was to swing off the porch rail out over the pond, let go of the gunnysack, and drop into the deepest part of the pond with a fine, cool splash.

I looked around after they ran over The Proper Villain, or rather his grave. There had been the usual harsh clatter and clank followed by the screech of rubber bruising itself against metal. If it had been going five miles per hour faster, the car might have broken a shock absorber or two and maybe even an axle.

But that was what The Proper Villain's grave was for—to make cars slow down so that they wouldn't run over our five dogs, eight cats, two goats, six ducks, and a pair of the meanest peacocks in three states and probably the District of Columbia.

When alive The Proper Villain had been a nine-year-old

yellow tomcat, alley born and bred somewhere in the freak haven that then lay just east of Dupont Circle in Washington. I had found him late one night in the alley back of the Sulgrave Club on Massachusetts Avenue. I had almost stepped on him and he had spit at me and swatted at my ankle, and the girl I was with, a Londoner from around Maida Vale, or maybe it was Paddington, had giggled and said, "Now there's a proper villain, isn't he?" At the time he was six weeks old. Maybe seven.

The Proper Villain lived five years in the carriage house in Washington and four more on the farm near Harpers Ferry before the Sears service truck flattened him on the quarter-mile dirt lane that led from the road to the house. It was the last time I ever bought anything from Sears.

I buried him on the spot, in the middle of the lane, and to mark his grave I built a bump out of rocks, dirt, and some old railroad ties that I found in Charles Town. The bump was a deceptively rounded ridge that stretched across the lane, but if you went over it at more than ten miles per hour, you were in for some front-end work.

Later, still mildly obsessed, I built twenty more of the bumps about fifty feet apart and put up signs reading "Five Miles Per Hour—This Means You" and "Posted—No Hunting" and "Keep Out—Trespassers Will Be Prosecuted" and "Beware of Vicious Dogs." Nobody ever paid any attention to the signs, of course, but they all slowed down to a crawl after they ran over The Proper Villain.

The car that had turned in was a new Mercedes 450 SEL sedan that had that rented or leased look to it. You can always tell. The driver was negotiating the lane cautiously now but I couldn't see who it was because the afternoon sun bounced off the windshield creating a glare. Still, I kept on watching until the car disappeared beneath the pines in front of the house.

I went back to tying the last square knot into the swing's rope and I remember thinking that perhaps I should get a book and teach myself to tie at least one or two other kinds when Ruth came out on the porch and looked up.

"You've got visitors," she said.

"I have or we have?"

"You have. Mr. Murfin and Mr. Quane."

"Ah."

"Yes," she said. "Ah."

"Well, maybe you'd better tell them I'm not here."

"I already told them that you are."

I thought about it for a moment. "Okay. On the porch. We'll do it on the porch."

"You want a little something?"

I thought again, trying to remember. "Bourbon," I said. "They both drink bourbon."

"The good bourbon or the other?"

"The other."

"That's what I thought," she said and went back into the house.

Murfin and Quane came out on the porch and looked around—to their left, their right, then down, and everywhere but up. I watched them for several seconds, maybe even as many as ten, thinking that they both were older and heavier and even greyer, but carrying their triple burden fairly well, all things considered, although it would take much more than ten seconds to consider all things.

"Up here," I said and then they both looked up a little surprised.

"Harvey," Murfin said and then Quane said, "How the hell are you?"

"Okay," I said. "And you?"

"Not bad," Murfin said and Quane said that he was all right, too.

We looked at each other some more. What I saw were two men in their late thirties whom I had known for twelve years but hadn't seen for three, possibly four. That made Ward Murfin about thirty-eight or thirty-nine. Max Quane was younger, probably thirty-seven. It was the middle of August and hot and neither of them wore coats, but they both wore shirts and ties although the ties were loosened. Murfin's shirt was pale green and Quane's was white with thin black stripes and a tab collar. I remembered then that he had always worn tab collars with a neat little gold pin in them.

"A swing, huh?" Murfin said.

"Uh-huh," I said.

Murfin quickly saw how it would work. "Right off the porch. Right off the rail here and then out over the pond. Shit, I'd like to try that."

"Why not?" I said and started climbing down the tree. I had to go hand over hand along the final branch and then drop about three feet onto the porch rail and balance there without falling. I did it quickly and smoothly, showing off, I suppose, and I could see both Murfin and Quane watching carefully, probably hoping that I'd fall on my ass, and perhaps even wondering if they could do it like that after maybe a bit of practice. I decided not to tell them how many times I'd practised it.

We shook hands then and they both still had their quick, firm, professional handshakes—the kind that preachers, politicians and most labour organizers have. After that was over I told them to sit anywhere and they decided on two canvas chairs, the kind that they call director's chairs in Hollywood and safari chairs in Africa. I'm not quite sure what they're called in Virginia.

I chose the bench swing, which was the old-fashioned kind suspended from the porch ceiling by thin metal chains. We sat there for a moment inspecting each other, probably for signs of dotage and infirmity, and none of us would have been unhappy at the discovery of a tremulous jowl here or a mild tic there.

Finally Murfin said, "I like your moustache."

I gave it a couple of strokes before I could stop myself. "I've had it a couple of years," I said. "Ruth says she likes it."

"It makes you look something like that old-time movie actor," Quane said. "Hell, he's dead now and I can't even remember his name, but he used to be in a lot of pictures with—uh—Myrna Loy."

"William Powell," Ruth said as she came out on to the porch with the tray. She put the tray down on the huge old wooden industrial cable spool that we used as a porch table. "It makes him look very much like Mr. Powell in *My Man Godfrey*, although I don't think Miss Loy was in that particular film."

That was how my wife talked about almost everybody, with a kind of grave, gentle formality that I found reassuring and others found disarming and even quaint. She was one of the few persons in the country who, despite her deep personal revulsion, had never referred to him as anything but Mr. Nixon. People sometimes asked me if she were always like that, even in private, and I assured them that she was although I could have added, but didn't, that in private we giggled a lot.

Ruth's excuse for leaving after she put the tray on the table was a charming lie about how she had to drive into Harpers Ferry for something that she had forgotten. I would have believed her myself except that she was one of those persons who almost never forgot anything. But her excuse made both Murfin and Quane preen a little because she made it sound as if she were regretfully forgoing what promised to prove the most fascinating afternoon of her life.

The tray that she had placed on the table contained three glasses, a bucket of ice, a pitcher of water, some fresh mint, and a quart of Virginia Gentleman, which is a bourbon distilled not far from Herndon and has something of a local following.

Neither Murfin nor Quane wanted any mint in their drinks so I mixed two without and one with. After we had all taken our first swallows, Murfin looked around, nodded approvingly at what he could see from the porch, and said, "You sure got it fixed up nice. I never thought you'd ever get it looking like this." He turned to Quane. "I was with him when he bought it; I ever tell you that?"

"About six times," Quane said. "Maybe seven."

"When was it," Murfin said to me, "eleven years ago?"

"Twelve," I said.

"Yeah, 1964. We'd just made that swing through the South about half a jump ahead of old Shorty Trope and he finally catches up with us in New Orleans and, Jesus, is he mad. Jumping up and down, all four foot eleven of him, half drunk like always, and yelling about how he's gonna clean both our ploughs good." Murfin gave his head a small, regretful shake. "Shorty's dead now. You know that?"

"I didn't know," I said.

"Died a couple of years ago in an old folks' home down in Savannah. Somehow he gets one of the niggers to bring him a jug. Old Cabin Still, I hear. Pays the nigger twenty dollars. Maybe twenty-five. They're not sure cause the nigger lied, of course. Well, Shorty'd been off the booze for a couple of years on account of his heart, but he gets this fifth and drinks her down in a couple of hours and then passes out and dies dead drunk and probably happy."

"Probably," I said.

"How old was he by then," Quane said, "sixty?"

"Sixty-three," said Murfin, who always liked to have all the details, even down to the amount of the fatal bribe. It was probably what made him good at what he did.

He went on with his tale, Quane only half listening now because by his own count this would be the eighth time that he'd heard it. Murfin told how he and I had flown out of New Orleans about two in the morning, both of us more than a little drunk, and still nowhere near sober when we landed at Dulles at six, and how I'd bought a copy of the *Washington Post* and read the ad and then had insisted that he drive me all the way out here, although it really wasn't much more than half an hour from Dulles. From Washington it was an hour. Often a little more.

"It sure as shit didn't look like much then, did it, Harvey?"

"Not much," I said.

"Well, by God, we walked all over it, over all eighty acres with this old guy who owned it—what was his name? Started with a P."

"Pasjk," I said. "Emil Pasjk."

"Yeah, Pasjk," Murfin said. "Well, this old man Pasjk says he wants three-fifty an acre and Harvey here dickers with him and then goes out to the car and comes back with a bottle of gin, Dixie Belle, I remember, and they dicker some more and by ten o'clock in the morning the gin's half gone and the old man's down to three hundred an acre so Longmire here whips out his chequebook and writes a twenty-four-hundred-dollar bum cheque for the down payment. How much you have in the bank then, Harvey?''

"About what I've got now," I said. "Three hundred. Maybe three fifty."

"It must be worth a hell of a lot more than that now," Quane said.

"Shoot," Murfin said, "you could probably get twenty-five hundred an acre for it now, couldn't you?"

"Maybe," I said.

Quane took another swallow of his drink and looked around. He was still looking away from me when he said, "We've got an idea that maybe might interest you."

"Uh-huh," I said and I must not have been able to keep it out of my voice, whatever it was, probably suspicion, maybe even dread, because Murfin caught it, countered it with a deprecatory gesture, and said, "I swear it's nothing like the last one."

"The last one," I said, perhaps a little dreamily. "I remember the last one. A rare gem of an idea. Maybe even one without price. It's still kind of hard to decide. I remember that I had to get all dressed up in a suit and tie and drive into Washington and have lunch at the Jockey Club and drink four martinis while I listened to your invitation to hop on the bandwagon for twelve hundred and fifty a week plus expenses. It was January thirteenth, as I recall, 1972. That was the last one you guys came up with. Wilbur Mills for President. Jesus."

Quane grinned. "Yeah, that one didn't work out too well, but the money was good."

"How long did it last?" I said.

Quane looked at Murfin. "Couple of months, wasn't it?"

"About that," Murfin said. "Then everybody found out that it wasn't a boom after all. What it was was sort of a popcorn fart."

"But now you've got something else," I said to Murfin.

"Something that lets you drive a leased Mercedes and keeps Quane here in hundred-dollar loafers."

Quane put a foot up on the table and let us admire one of his loafers. The right one. "Hell of a shoe," he said.

"We sort of fell into the honeypot, me and Quane," Murfin said.

"What's the honeypot's name?" I said.

Murfin grinned. It was his hard, nasty, pleased grin—not quite vicious, and although I had seen it often enough before it never failed to make me want to look away—as though I had been given a quick peek at some awful private deformity that was really none of my business. "Roger Vullo," he said.

"Well," I said.

"Vullo Pharmaceuticals," Murfin said.

"I know. How old is he now?"

Murfin looked at Quane. "Twenty-nine?"

Quane nodded. "About that."

"What's he up to this time?" I said. "The last I heard he was trying to buy himself a Congress."

"Did pretty good, too," Murfin said. "He spent maybe a million or so and ninety-six per cent of the ones he backed got elected and it was gonna be veto-proof, except it didn't quite work out like that, and Vullo got a little disillusioned with politics."

"I'm sorry to hear that," I said. "At least I think I am."

"Vullo came up with something else," Quane said.

I nodded. "One should keep busy."

"We've been setting it up for him," Quane said.

I nodded again. "He chose well."

"Us and the lawyers and some computer people."

"It sounds fat," I said.

"It is," Murfin said.

"What've you been setting up, you and the lawyers and the computer people?"

"It's a kind of foundation," Quane said.

"Something to do with good works," I said. "And taxes, too, I imagine. Good works and taxes often seem to go hand in hand. What's the foundation to be called?"

"The Arnold Vullo Foundation," Murfin said.

"Touching," I said. "After his late father."

"Grandfather, too," Quane said. "The grandfather's name was Arnold."

"Also the elder brother as I remember," I said. "I mean Roger's elder brother. He was Arnold Vullo the third. All three of them, wasn't it, plus the mother. I mean all three Arnold Vullos, plus Mrs. Arnold Vullo the second, were killed in that private plane crash leaving poor Roger at what, twenty-one, the sole heir to perhaps two hundred million or thereabouts?"

"Thereabouts," Quane said.

"They never did find out who put the bomb in the plane, did they?" I said.

"Never did," Murfin said.

"Young Roger was upset, as I recall," I said. "He went around making public statements about shoddy police work. I think he said shoddy."

"In private he said shitty," Murfin said. "Shoddy was what he used in all those press releases he put out. And that's what the foundation's all about."

"Shitty police work?" I said. "A ripe field. Very ripe."

"He's narrowed it down," Quane said.

"To what?"

"Conspiracy."

"Christ," I said, "who sold him on that? You two? I'm not saying that you don't know a lot about conspiracy. I mean, if I wanted to put one together—you know, a really first-class job—I'd certainly come to you guys."

"Funny," Quane said, "that's just what Ward and I were saying on the way out here. About you, I mean."

We sat there on the porch in silence for a moment. And then, almost on cue, we each took another swallow of our drinks. Quane lit a cigarette. A mockingbird cut loose nearby with a shrill series of his latest impressions. Somewhere one of the dogs barked once, a lazy, half-hearted bark. Honest Tuan, the Siamese, stalked out onto the porch as if he thought he might have some business with the mockingbird. He changed his mind abruptly and decided that what he really wanted to do was flop down and yawn, which he did.

I reached over and borrowed a cigarette from Quane's pack. He still smoked Camels, I noticed. I lit the cigarette and said, "The Kennedys. He's going to stir all that up again, isn't he?"

Murfin nodded. "He already has. Maybe you've noticed."

"I've noticed," I said. "Who else? King? Wallace?" Murfin nodded again.

"That's four," I said, "and all the crap that happened afterward. Anybody else?"

"Hoffa," Quane said.

"Jesus," I said. "Jimmy's almost still warm."

"We figure that'll be the easiest one," Murfin said. "It's kind of obvious, isn't it?"

"Kind of," I said.

"There's one more," Quane said. "Yours."

"Mine?"

"Uh-huh. Yours. Arch Mix."

The mockingbird abruptly shut up. There was no sound for a moment, no sound at all, and then a trout jumped in the pond. I rattled the ice in my glass. Then I said, "Never."

"Ten thousand," Murfin said quickly. "Ten thousand for two months' work. If you turn it, another ten thousand."

"No."

"You know why we're handing it to you, don't you?" Murfin said. "I mean, you knew Mix better'n anybody else. Christ, you didn't do anything but study him for what, five months?"

"Six," I said. "I grew old studying him. When it was over I came down with mono. That's silly, isn't it? A thirty-two-year-old man with mono."

"Harvey," Murfin said. "Talk to Vullo, will you? That's all. Just talk to him. We told him we really didn't expect you to turn up the who on Mix, but maybe you could come up with the why. If we got that, the why, then me and Quane could turn some redhots we got loose on the who."

"You think there is a who, don't you?" I said.

"There's gotta be," Murfin said and Quane nodded wisely. "Look," Murfin went on, selling me now, "a guy has a great job. He gets along with his wife—well, okay anyway. His health's good. He's forty-five and his kids aren't in jail and that's something. So he gets up one morning, has breakfast, reads the paper, gets in his car and starts to work. He never gets there. They never find him. They never even find his car. He's just gone."

"It happens all the time," I said. "Every week. Maybe every day. It's called the 'Honey, I Think I'll Run Down to the Drugstore for Some Cigarettes' syndrome."

"Mix didn't smoke," said Murfin, the stickler.

"You're right. I forgot."

"Harvey," Quane said.

"What?"

"Five hundred bucks. Just to talk to Roger Vullo."

I got up and went over to the porch rail. I took off my shirt and jeans. Underneath I was wearing some swimming trunks. I picked up the long bamboo pole with the hook on the end that I'd made out of a coat hanger. I used the hook to pull the rope swing in, grasped the gunnysack, and climbed up on the porch rail. I turned. Murfin and Quane were watching me. So was Honest Tuan.

"A thousand," I said. "I'll talk to him for a thousand."

I shoved off of the porch rail and sailed out over the pond. At the top of the swing's arc I let go and started falling. When I hit the water I made a fine big splash and it was as much fun as I had thought it would be. Maybe even more.

2

In my youth, which I sometimes enjoy thinking of as misspent, I was a bit of an over-achiever in a limited kind of way. Or perhaps I was simply in a hurry although a bit unsure of my destination. If any. But by the time I was thirty-two I had been a student, a police reporter, a state legislator, a foreign correspondent, a political gunslinger, and some even thought, mistakenly, a secret agent of sorts. Now at forty-three I was a poetaster and a goatherd, providing that two Nubian goats could be considered a herd.

I learned my political primer in the New Orleans French Quarter where I was born, reared (rather loosely in retrospect), and whose crime I eventually covered for the old *Item*, a newspaper that I went to work for at seventeen while attending Tulane University. My studies were less than arduous since I majored in French and German, two languages that I learned to speak before I was five because my mother had been born in Dijon, my father in Düsseldorf.

In 1954, when I was twenty-one and just graduated, some of the more depraved elements in the quarter decided in a fit of political pique, defiance, and probably despair that they should send a bitter joke to Baton Rouge as their state representative. They sent me. I won handily as a kind of machine candidate and achieved no little notoriety by making a good solemn campaign promise which was to introduce a bill that would legalize cunnilingus and fellatio between consenting adults. Needless to say (then why say it?) my political career died swiftly and my self-appointed mentor, a kindly, ageing former crony of the sainted Huey Long, advised me in all seriousness that, "Harvey, the state just ain't quite ready for a pussy-eatin' bill yet."

But a state legislature is an excellent place to further one's political education, and if one is particularly interested in the study of political chicanery, knavery, improbity, and bamboozlement, the Louisiana state legislature was then— and may yet be—the *fons et origo* of all such knowledge. After my single term there I was never again to be shocked or surprised by political rascality. Saddened a few times and amused often, but shocked never.

For no very good reason, I was thinking about my tarnished past as I stood before the mirror in the bathroom trying to decide whether to shave off my moustache. Ruth went by in the hall, stopped, and leaned against the door jamb.

"If you shave it off," she said, "you won't look like Mr. Powell anymore."

I put a finger up trying to block out the moustache. "But there'd be a startling resemblance to Victor McLaglen, wouldn't there?"

She looked at me critically. "Perhaps," she said, "especially if you learned how to twist a cloth cap in your hands. He could twist a cloth cap better than anyone."

"Well, hell," I said, "I think I'll leave it."

"What time are you supposed to see Mr. Vullo?"

"Eleven. You need anything?"

"Gin," she said. "We're low on gin. And I also need three birthdays, a tenth and twentieth wedding anniversary, two get wells, a congratulations for a five-to-seven-year-old, and a couple of miss you's."

About half our income—which the previous year had reached a staggering $11,763—came from the sale of Ruth's watercolour drawings to a Los Angeles greeting card firm. She drew gentle, immensely clever caricatures of animals and her models were mostly members of our own menagerie—

plus a couple of beavers who lived upstream from the pond and for the most part minded their own business. The Los Angeles firm couldn't get enough of Ruth's drawings.

Quite by accident I had found that I had a remarkable talent for writing greeting card verse that contained just the right touch of simpering banality. The L.A. firm paid me two dollars a line and occasionally dropped me warm little notes that compared my efforts favourably with those of Rod McKuen. I did a lot of composing while milking the goats. Birthdays were my speciality.

I told Ruth that I'd write the stuff on my way to Washington. I had also discovered that while driving I could usually compose a line a mile. In the bedroom I opened a closet and studied the remnants of a once fairly resplendent wardrobe. Time, fashion, and personal indifference had reduced it to one London-tailored suit (the last of six), which I planned to be cremated in, a couple of tweed jackets, some jeans, and a seersucker suit with suspicious labels. I chose the seersucker, a blue shirt, a black knit tie, and when I looked into the mirror I thought I looked quite natty—providing that one still thought of 1965 as a natty year.

I drove the pickup into Washington. It was a 1969 Ford with a four-wheel drive, which came in handy when it snowed or rained. I left our other car for Ruth. Our other car was a five-year-old Volkswagen.

By the time I arrived at Connecticut Avenue and M Street I had composed thirty-six lines of doggerel, which I dictated into a small portable tape recorder, shouting some of the lines, even declaiming them to make myself heard above the Ford's clatter. They rhymed, they scanned, and they were as sticky as honey and twice as sweet.

I treated myself to one of those dollar-and-a-quarter-an-hour parking lots and then found the M Street address that Murfin had given me. It was a fairly new building just east of Connecticut Avenue on the south side of the street. I rode the elevator up to the sixth floor, walked down the hall, and went through a door that was lettered: THE ARNOLD VULLO FOUNDATION.

On the other side of the door was a young receptionist

and behind her was a rather large area filled with metal desks that were separated from each other by thin, pastel partitions that rose about five feet above the floor. The partitions were light tan, pale blue, and dusty rose. At the desks sat about two dozen men and women, most of them in their late twenties, although some were older, who typed, read, talked into phones, or simply sat staring into space. It looked very much like the city room of a prosperous medium-sized daily newspaper.

I told the receptionist that my name was Harvey Longmire and that I had an appointment with Mr. Murfin. She nodded, picked up the phone, dialled a few numbers, said something into it, and then smiled at me as she hung up.

"Won't you take a seat, Mr. Longmire? Somebody'll be here in a moment to show you to Mr. Murfin's office."

I took a seat and looked around at the reception area. It was all good, solid furniture that had a kind of W&J Sloane look to it. It was as if whoever had chosen it had decided on stolid durability and comfort rather than flash. I looked at my watch and saw that I was ten minutes early, but then I usually am, so I took out my small tin box and rolled a cigarette. I once smoked three packs of cigarettes a day. Luckys, unfiltered, but since I had started rolling my own I was down to the equivalent of a pack a day for which my lungs seemed grateful. I also saved approximately $124 a year.

I could sense the receptionist watching me so I decided to give her a thrill and rolled the cigarette with one hand. I looked up at her and grinned. "I used to be a cowpoke," I said.

"You never," she said, smiling. "I wish I could do that."

"You don't smoke, do you?"

She smiled again. "Not tobacco. That is tobacco, isn't it?"

"Afraid so," I said.

The receptionist went back to doing what she was doing when I came in, proofreading, it seemed, and I went back to smoking my roll-your-own. I was about halfway through it when a door opened and a tall woman with streaked blonde hair came in and said, "Mr. Longmire?"

I said that I was Longmire and she said that she was Mr. Murfin's secretary and that if I would follow her she would show me to Mr. Murfin's office and even get me a cup of coffee and how did I like it. I said I liked it with sugar.

I followed the woman with the streaked hair down a carpeted hall that had five or six doors leading off of it. All of the doors were closed. She stopped at one of them and opened it, indicating that I should go in. I went in and found Murfin behind a large desk and Quane seated on a couch, his feet up on the coffee table.

We didn't shake hands this time. Quane waved at me lazily and Murfin nodded and grinned and said, "You're right on time."

"Habit," I said. "My only good one."

"Ginger'll get you some coffee," Murfin said.

"Ginger's the blonde?"

"My secretary."

I looked around at Murfin's office and nodded. "They seem to do you well here."

Murfin also looked around and nodded, a little possessively, I thought, at the good-sized room with its dark brown carpet, fabric-covered walls, long sofa, four easy chairs, the coffee table, and what looked like a bar in one corner although it could have been a cleverly disguised filing cabinet. There were even some tasteful prints on the walls, but I was sure that Murfin hadn't selected them because Murfin had no taste.

"I've had worse," Murfin said. "A lot worse."

"I know."

"Vullo's gonna be tied up for about ten minutes so I thought we'd have coffee first and then I'd take you in and introduce you."

"What about the money?" I said.

"No problem."

"He means he wants it in advance," Quane said. "Right?"

"Right," I said.

"Jesus, Harvey," Murfin said, "you don't hardly change at all."

"In our changing world constancy is a treasure."

Ginger, the secretary, came in with a tray containing three cups of coffee. There were even saucers and spoons to go with the cups. She served me first and then Quane and then Murfin. When she was done, Murfin said, "Bring that Longmire cheque in, will you Ginger?"

She nodded, left, and came back a few moments later with a cheque which she handed to Murfin. He thanked her and when she was gone he took out a ball-point pen and signed the cheque and then slid it over to Quane who used the same pen to sign his name. Quane then handed the cheque to me. I looked at it and put it in the breast pocket of my jacket.

"You guys sign the cheques around here?" I said.

Murfin nodded. "Some of them. I sign them and Quane here countersigns them."

"That's good," I said. "They've got the fox watching the weasel. That's very clever."

We all took a sip of our coffee and I noticed that Murfin still slurped his after blowing on it first. I decided that he hadn't changed much since I had first met him twelve years before. He had put on a few pounds, but not many, and his dark brown hair was greying a little, but he still had his round pink face, almost unlined, his stubby nose, apple chin, wide, thin mouth with its mean smile, and eyes that were shaded a merciless blue.

Now that he was all dressed up I had nearly forgotten how awful his clothes always were, but that came back as I examined his brown and green plaid summer-weight jacket, pink shirt, and the red, white and yellow tie that dribbled down its front something like a tomato surprise.

It was Quane who had changed more. He was nearly as tall as I, almost six feet, but he looked leaner and his face had lost its chubby youthfulness and was now all planes, angles and harsh lines that were almost slashes. A couple of lines were deep parenthetical grooves that ran down from the sides of his beaky nose to the corners of his mouth, which still looked as if it wanted to pout or maybe bitch about something.

I remembered that Quane's eyes when I had first seen them had been wide and grey and brimming over with something moist, probably innocence. They were still grey, of course, but they seemed to have narrowed and the moist innocence had all dried up and gone away. It was hard to tell what had taken its place. Probably nothing.

"Well," I said, "then what happened? You never did tell me."

"When?" Quane said.

"After Wilbur Mills."

Murfin shook his head. "It was a rotten year. We hooked up with Muskie and then Humphrey and after the convention we landed a couple of advance spots with Eagleton."

"You're right," I said. "It was a rotten year."

"So after the Eagleton thing," Murfin said, "well, hell, I just went home and sat around the house and drove Marjorie and the kids crazy."

"How is Marjorie?" I said, trying to put a little interest into my question, but not succeeding too well. Marjorie was probably as nutty as ever.

"She's a pain in the ass," Murfin said. "She's started going to one of those consciousness-raising things twice a week. Now I don't hardly ever want to go home."

"Well, some things never change," I said. "That brings us up to Watergate. I heard both of you landed somewhere on the committee."

"I did first," Murfin said, "and then I finally got hold of Quane."

"Where were you?"

"Mexico," Quane said.

"Tell him about Mexico," Murfin said.

"There's nothing to tell," Quane said.

Murfin licked his lips and smiled one of his more terrible smiles. "They had this B-26," he said. "Quane and a couple of other guys and this sixty-one-year-old World War Two-type pilot who claimed he could fly the goddamned thing. Or he was supposed to be able to fly it when he was sober anyhow, which was maybe every fourth day for about six hours. Well, they've got six tons of dope. Can you imagine, six tons? And they're gonna fly it into the desert somewhere in Arizona and everybody's gonna get rich. Well, they sober the old Air Corps vet up, and he finally finds his bifocals someplace and puts those on, and they've got the plane all loaded and everything's set, except there's just one little thing wrong. The goddamned engines won't start.''

"So what happened?" I said.

Quane shrugged. "The last time I looked back they were still trying to start them. I only looked back once."

"And that's when you went on the Watergate committee?" I said.

"As consultants," Murfin said. "We got one twenty-eight a day and an office and some pencils and some yellow pads and what we did was think up questions. We thought up some pretty good ones."

"The tapes," I said. "I think I heard somewhere from somebody that it was you guys who really came up with the question about the tapes."

Murfin looked at Quane who said nothing but merely smiled a little.

"It was a pretty good question," I said.

Quane nodded. "Not bad."

"It only lasted till October though," Murfin said.

"Of seventy-three?"

"Yeah."

"Then what?"

"Well," Murfin said, "by then I'm off the payroll and I'm looking around again, you know trying to connect somewhere, and about the only offer I get is from the Teamsters who wanta know if I'd like to go out to California and help red-dog Chavez. Well, shit, I mean, who wants to do that?"

"Besides," I said, "it might be hard work."

"Exactly. Well, finally I sort of stumble over this guy out in Ohio who thinks he wants to be a congressman, and his wife thinks so, too, and money's no problem because they've both got a ton of it, and about the only problem they got is that they don't quite know how to go about getting elected."

"Musacco," I said. "You dumped Nick Musacco."

I was given another quick look at Murfin's awful smile. He could flick it on and off like a flashlight. "Yeah," he said. "Nick was about due, don'tcha think?"

I shrugged. "Ten years ago," I said, "maybe even five, Nick would have skinned you and hung you out to dry before breakfast. Or maybe lunch."

Murfin moved his shoulders indifferently. "He got old. Old and slow and careless. So anyhow, I pulled in Quane here on that one and our new congressman and his wife got all excited and happy, especially his wife because by then I'm balling her kind of regular at the Holiday Inn just up the street on Rhode Island." He jerked his head in the direction of the motel. "And the new congressman's begging me to stay on as his A.A."

"But you didn't," I said.

"Well, hell, can you see me as some freshman congressman's administrative assistant?"

"No," I said. "I suppose not. Not really."

"Anyway," Murfin went on, "I set up his office for him and pointed him toward the Capitol in case he wanted to vote sometime and he's so grateful for everything that he slips me a five-thousand cash money bonus out of his own pocket, but makes me promise not to tell his wife, which I sure as shit didn't on account of she'd already slipped me two thousand herself. Cash money."

I looked at Quane. "He split with you?"

"Kind of," Quane said. "One third, two thirds. Guess who got the one third?"

Murfin gave us another one of his smiles and once again I didn't quite look away. "You didn't have to fuck his wife," he told Quane. "I did."

"And after that what'd you do?" I said.

Murfin looked at Quane. Quane only smiled. "This and that," Murfin said.

I decided not to ask what this and that was. I decided that

I really didn't want to know. "But after all the this and that Vullo came looking for you, right?"

"Right," Murfin said. "He was looking for somebody who could organize this thing and then run it and that's what Quane and I are good at."

They were indeed good at that, plus a few other things, so I nodded my agreement. "What do all those people out there with the coloured desks do?" I said.

"That's the staff, or most of it, except for the comptroller and his people, the computer types, the legal counsel, Vullo, me and Quane here. We got some of the ones you saw out there from the *Post* and the *Star*. We stole maybe three or four from Nader. A couple are from *The Wall Street Journal*. About a half dozen are lawyers and another two or three used to be cops. Detectives. We even got one guy from the FBI."

"And they're going to sniff out conspiracy?" I said.

"Wherever it exists," Quane said. "Or existed."

"When you come up with something, what'll you do with it?"

"Well, we're gonna be a sort of clearing house and we're also gonna put out a monthly magazine," Murfin said. "That's what they're doing out there now, putting together a dummy issue. When everything's all set it'll sell for twenty or twenty-five bucks a year and for that you also become a member of the Foundation. And the twenty or twenty-five bucks or whatever will be deductible."

"We stole that from the *National Geographic*," Quane said.

"What're you going to call yours?" I said. "*The Paranoia Review*?"

"Nah," Murfin said. "I came up with the title, as a matter of fact. We're gonna call it *The Vullo Report*."

"That's catchy."

"Vullo likes it," Quane said.

"I bet."

There was a pause and then Murfin cleared his throat and said, "Harvey."

"What?"

"Vullo thinks Quane here and me are pretty hot shit."

"So do I."

"I mean he doesn't know—well, every last detail about us."

I smiled politely and said nothing.

"What I'm saying," Murfin went on, "is that this is a pretty nice deal and we don't want it fucked up."

"You should know by now that I won't dump on you."

Murfin smiled his blackguard's smile again. "Well, hell, we know that. I just thought I'd mention it."

"How much does Vullo know about me?"

This time Murfin frowned and it made him look serious and grave and almost guileless. But not quite. "Well, you know, we had to tell him quite a bit."

"What's quite a bit," I said, "everything?"

"Damn near," Quane said.

"And what did Vullo say?"

Murfin quit frowning and started smiling. I almost wished that he had gone on frowning. "He said he thought you sounded fascinating."

"Well, what the hell," I said. "I am."

3

Roger Vullo bit his fingernails. He bit them so often and so thoroughly that the quicks had moved down at least a quarter of an inch from the tips of his fingers. In fact, he had very little nail left and I concluded he must have been biting them all his life.

I probably had read somewhere why people bite their fingernails, but I couldn't recall it so I resolved to look it up. I also decided that while I was at it I would see whether I could find out something about another bad habit, which was the one that Mary Jane Wynne had had in the fourth grade, although hers may have been unique.

Mary Jane picked her nose and saved the treasures in a penny matchbox. She took them home after school, put sugar on them, and ate them. It should have been a secret vice, but Mary Jane bragged about it, and all of us in the fourth grade were very much in awe of her.

I was noticing Vullo's fingernails and thinking about Mary Jane so I didn't pay much attention to what Vullo and Murfin were saying because they were discussing some administrative problem. I perked up only when Vullo said, "That's all, Murfin. Out."

It was a peremptory dismissal, rude in its curtness, arrogant in its phrasing, and delivered in a tone that is usually reserved for dismissing army privates, indentured servants, and maybe even rotten little kids.

Murfin had brought me into Vullo's office, introduced us, and I had sat down in a chair although nobody had invited me to. Murfin had remained standing while he and Vullo discussed their problem and I had admired Vullo's fingernails and remembered Mary Jane.

Now Murfin had been abruptly dismissed and I thought I saw his back stiffen. But when he turned to leave he winked and grinned at me so I assumed that Vullo spoke to all the help like that and probably had since he was five.

I decided that Roger Vullo had treated himself to either the fifth or sixth largest office in Washington, possibly even the fourth. It also looked as though the decorator had been admonished to fill the room with an air of rich, permanent grandeur and hang the cost. Vullo ran things from behind a huge, gleaming desk that was at least two centuries old. During all those years it must have been waxed daily. Perhaps even twice daily. Jutting out from the desk was a narrow refectory table, long enough for two dozen Spanish monks to have dined around once, possibly five hundred years ago. I assumed that it was now used for staff conferences.

The rest of the furniture was mostly solid, leather stuff, including the chair that I sat in, the sixteen chairs around the refectory table, the divan against one wall, and the three wing-backed chairs that went with it. The place had the pleasant, mildly pungent smell of a shoe repair shop.

On the floor was a thick beige carpet and covering the walls was something that looked like pale burlap, but probably wasn't because burlap would have been too cheap. One wall was lined with old leatherbound books, but I was too far away to read their titles. The wall opposite the books was hung with a series of Daumier drawings, six in all, and for all I knew they may have been the originals. Vullo could probably afford them. I rapidly was becoming convinced that he could afford almost anything.

The only thing that clashed with the decor was Vullo himself and, now that I think about it, me. After Murfin had gone Vullo sat slumped in his chair behind the immense desk staring at me coolly, maybe even coldly, with narrowed hazel eyes that seemed shrewd, clever, and possibly even brilliant. He quit staring only when he remembered that it was time to bite his fingernails.

He gave his right thumb a couple of fierce nips, admired the results, and said, "You live on a farm now." It was an accusation the way he said it.

I decided that I might as well confess, so I said, "That's right."

"Near Harpers Ferry."

"Yes."

"John Brown."

"Lee, too."

"Lee?"

"Robert E. Lee," I said. "He was a US colonel then and he led the detachment of marines that wounded Brown and then captured him."

"I didn't remember that it was Lee."

"Not everybody does."

"They hanged him, didn't they?"

"Brown? They hanged him all right. They captured him on October eighteenth and hanged him on December second."

"What year was that?"

"1859?"

"He was quite mad, wasn't he? Brown."

I thought about it for a moment. "Everybody says so, but I'm not so sure. He was a fanatic anyway and maybe all fanatics are a little nuts. Crazy or not, they hanged him."

Vullo abruptly lost interest in John Brown. He went back to me. "What do you grow on your farm?"

"Vegetables, clover, goats, honey, and Christmas trees."

Vullo nodded as if all that were perfectly logical. But he needed more details. He would probably always need more details and that may have been why he had hired Murfin. They were two kindred spirits who could feast on a handful of details.

Suddenly Vullo frowned and it made him appear dubious and even a bit petulant. He looked as if he had just found out that I had lied to him. He had a lean, hollowed-out face with a bony chin and a nose so sharp and thin that I wondered if he had trouble breathing through it. His cheekbones seemed to be straining to be let out and his mouth was a small, pale, tight line about an inch long. It was a sullen, pinched-in face, wary and bitter, the kind that is sometimes worn either by slum kids or very rich old men.

"You don't raise honey," he said, catching me out in my lie.

"No," I said, "you keep bees. We have four hives."

"What kind of honey do they make?"

"Clover honey with a little goldenrod mixed in. It's light-coloured and mild although the goldenrod adds a bit of tang."

"Do they sting you?"

"Sometimes."

"I've never been stung by a bee. Does it hurt?"

I shrugged. "You get used to it. You build up an immunity and after a while they don't bother you. The stings, I mean. The first thing you learn is not to wear blue jeans. Bees hate blue jeans."

Now that was a detail he really liked. He liked it so much that he jotted it down on a pad. While he was making his note, he said, "How many goats do you keep?"

"Two."

"How much milk can you get from two goats?"

"About four hundred gallons a year," I said. "A little over a gallon a day."

"You don't drink that much, do you?"

"No. We make our own cheese and butter. The butter's good, but the cheese isn't so hot. It's supposed to be a Brie, but it's not turning out quite right, probably because I can't keep the cellar at a steady fifty-five degrees."

"And the rest of the milk?"

"We feed it to our cats and dogs. They're crazy about it."

"You milk the goats yourself?"

"Sure."

"How often?"

"Twice a day. Once about eight and again about seven or seven-thirty."

"Chickens? You raise chickens?"

"No."

"Why not?"

"My wife thinks chickens are dumb. There's a man down the road who raises them. He trades us dressed hens and eggs for honey and butter and trout, but we make him catch his own. Trout, I mean."

"How long have you been living on your farm?"

"Four years. Since 1972."

"That was when you dropped out, wasn't it?"

"I didn't drop out."

"Retired."

"I didn't retire."

"What would you call it?"

"I don't have to call it anything."

Vullo had been leaning toward me, his elbows on the desk. He was wearing a suit, a cheap grey one that fitted him poorly and might have come from Penney's or even Robert Hall's. Its elbows were shiny, or at least shinier than the rest of the suit whose synthetic fibres had a glisten all of their own. Beneath the coat was a white shirt with a collar whose points went this way and that. The collar was plugged by the small knot of a narrow green and yellow tie that had some interesting spots on it. Catsup, I decided, and maybe a little dried cottage cheese.

Vullo stared at me some more, then ran his fingers through his thick brown hair that he wore the way most men wore their hair in 1959. After that he slumped back in his chair and flung his yellow pencil on the desk. It was a child's gesture. A peevish child.

"Tell me about you and the CIA," he said.

I reached inside my jacket pocket, touched the thousand-dollar cheque, and decided to tell him about my Uncle Slick.

His name wasn't really Uncle Slick, of course, it was Jean-Jacques Le Gouis and he was my mother's younger brother. The Le Gouis family had moved to the States from

Dijon in 1929 when my mother was eighteen and my uncle was nine. By 1941 my uncle was twenty-one and a senior at Yale, a fact that my father always found impossible to believe. It was my old man who first called Jean-Jacques "Slick" and the nickname had stuck, because that's what my uncle was. Slick. Some people have remarked that I look very much like him and I've never been quite sure how to take it.

My uncle had a very pleasant war with the OSS in England and France and afterward he stayed on with the CIA. In 1964 he showed up unexpectedly in Berlin where I was working for something called the Morningside Network. We did a nightly radio world news wrapup and sold it to independent stations in the States. I had left the *Item* to join it in 1959 and I worked sometimes out of Bonn and sometimes Berlin.

In 1961 I had been in the Congo for a while, about the time that Patrice Lumumba was getting his, and that had been the last time I had seen Uncle Slick, which was, I thought, a bit more than coincidental. I never was sure what Slick did for the CIA. Something nasty probably.

In Berlin he had taken me out to dinner, an expensive spot just off the Kurfürstendamm, as I recall, made his usual fuss about ordering the wine, and then said that my mother had written him that I was thinking of returning to the States. I told him that I was only thinking about it, mostly because five years abroad seemed about enough. My only problem was a job. I didn't have one lined up mostly, I liked to think, because I really hadn't tried.

Uncle Slick said that he had just happened to have heard of one in Washington that would last at least six months and might well turn out to be permanent. Not only that but it also paid eighteen thousand a year, which was six thousand more than I was making then. I said that I was mildly interested and asked what I would have to do. He said that all I needed to do was write a letter, setting forth my qualifications and experience, and he had some old friends who would put in a word for me. That's how these things worked, he assured me.

I told him that I was pretty well up on how things work. What I was really interested in was what I would be doing for whom. My uncle made me a very pretty little speech about how I would be helping keep a labour statesman in office. He was speaking English now and using his Louis Jourdan accent, which he always used when he was selling something, although he could, when he wanted to, speak in the mellow tones of Yale. When he wanted to be snotty he spoke English very much like Basil Rathbone.

The labour statesman, it turned out, was one Stacey Hundermark, who was president of something called the Public Employees Union (AFL-CIO), which Hundermark had helped found back in Minneapolis in 1932 and had since nurtured to a respectable membership of around 250,000. Now, it seemed, some young upstart wanted to take Hundermark's job away from him. The upstart was one Arch Mix who, my uncle had hastened to assure me, was no relation to Tom.

"Hundermark," Vullo said. "He's dead now, isn't he?"

"He died the year after Mix defeated him."

"That was when?"

"Mix beat him in 1964."

"You went to work for Hundermark when?"

"That same year. Sixty-four. Early sixty-four."

"What happened?"

"Mix squeaked in by eight votes at the convention. I could have bought the votes, if I had known they were up for sale, which I should have, but didn't."

"You had plenty of money."

"More than plenty."

"Didn't you ever wonder where it came from?"

I shrugged.

"It came from the CIA."

"So it would seem."

"Some people thought you were with the CIA," Vullo said. "Mix said so."

"He was wrong."

"You were what—a dupe?"

"Uh-huh," I said. "A dupe."

Vullo nodded dubiously as if he wanted me to know that he thought I was lying. I touched the cheque again for solace and then brought out my tin box and rolled a cigarette. I took my time and looked up at Vullo once. He was watching me with an expression of faint disapproval. I wasn't sure whether he disapproved of my smoking or of the fact that I rolled my own. After I lit the cigarette he reached into a drawer and produced a small glass ashtray, the kind that you can buy in a drugstore for twenty-nine cents. He shoved it across the desk to me.

"The CIA's real interest in Hundermark was that international thing he set up—what was it called?"

"The PWI," I said. "Public Workers International."

"It was sort of a loose confederation of all the public-employee unions of the world, wasn't it?"

"The free world," I said. "I think they were still calling it the free world back in the sixties."

"And the CIA financed that, too, didn't they?" Vullo said. "The PWI, I mean."

"A lot of it. They staffed it, too." I put my cigarette out in the ashtray. "There were two co-directors. One was a nice guy from Kilgore, Texas. The other was a Harvard type with six kids. They were always jumping off to someplace like Lagos or Singapore or Mauritius."

"And that was why the CIA wanted to make sure that Hundermark was re-elected," Vullo said. "So that they could keep on using the PWI."

"That's right," I said.

"They didn't think that Mix would go along with it if he got elected and found out?"

"They were right, too. The second thing that Mix did when he won the presidency was to dissolve the PWI, or at least dissolve the union's ties with it."

"What was the first thing he did?"

"He fired me—except that I'd already quit. But Mix fired me anyway, at least in the newspapers. Then he fired Murfin and Quane."

"Mix didn't care for you, did he?"

"No."

"Did you know him well?"

"Probably better than anybody, except possibly his wife. By that I mean that I had studied him—the way that you might study an insect or something that lies in a tidepool."

"You didn't like him?"

I shrugged. "I didn't like him or dislike him. I studied him so that I'd be able to predict his moves and his reactions to whatever moves I made."

"You make it sound like a chess game."

"It wasn't any game. It was more like a fight. Or a battle, I suppose."

"And you ran Hundermark's campaign?"

"With the help of Murfin and Quane. The rest of the staff were mostly hangers-on that Hundermark had accumulated over the years. They tended to panic."

"But Murfin and Quane didn't?"

"No. They're not the type to panic."

"Wasn't Hundermark of any help?"

I started to tell him about Hundermark, but then I decided not to. Hundermark was dead and Vullo was paying me to tell him about Mix, not Hundermark. But it came back to me then, at least some of it, especially the night that I had gone up to Hundermark's office to tell him there was a fifty-fifty chance that he was going to get dumped.

He had sat there at his desk, a portly, pleasant, soft-looking man with rimless glasses who had never been able to bring himself to be one of the boys. He was something of a joke at AFL-CIO headquarters. Meany had despised him and Reuther had pitied him and I hadn't been sure which was worse.

"I just talked to Murfin and Quane," I had said. "We haven't quite got it. We're about two or three votes short. Maybe even four."

Hundermark had nodded thoughtfully and smiled gently. "Oh, I think we'll be all right," he had said. Then he had reached into his inside pocket and brought out a letter and unfolded it. He had read the letter silently, nodding to himself in a curiously comfortable, gentle sort of way.

"This letter," he said, "is from my practitioner." Hundermark was a Christian Scientist.

"He assures me that the forces of good will overcome the forces of evil."

"Well," I'd said, "maybe you'd better see if those forces of good can scratch up another ten thousand dollars."

Hundermark had smiled gently again. "Well, yes, I'm sure that they will be able to do that."

The forces of good, although I didn't know it, had been the CIA, of course, and it had promptly come up with the ten thousand, all cash, which I had spent as wisely and well as I knew how. But the forces of evil won by four votes anyway and Hundermark was out of a job and sometimes I wondered if later he had ever discussed the mystery of it all with his practitioner.

Vullo didn't want to talk about Hundermark anymore. He wanted to talk about me. "What happened to you after you got fired?"

"I quit," I said.

"I mean quit."

"I came down with mononucleosis and got an offer to jump into a senatorial campaign to see whether I could turn it around in the last four weeks. Or maybe three. I did and the guy won and paid me a lot of money and I paid off most of my farm and went to England."

"What did you do in England?"

"I lay down for a long time until the mono went away."

"Then what?"

"I met my wife."

"Is she English?"

"No."

Vullo sat there as if he were waiting for me to tell him some more about Ruth, but when I didn't he gave up and said, "You came back from England when?"

"Sixty-six."

"And took on a couple of campaigns, I understand. One for the Senate and one for the House."

"That's right. Both sure losers."

"But they didn't lose."

"No."

"And you gained quite a reputation."

It wasn't a question so I didn't say anything.

"Between 1966 and 1972 you took on thirteen Congressional and Senatorial campaigns and won twelve of them and each of them was what virtually everyone considered to be what you call a sure loser. I'm curious how you did it."

"I knew where to look."

"For what?"

"Dead bodies."

"*Time* called you a political gunslinger."

"*Time* still gets a little vivid."

"And sometimes you hired Murfin and Quane."

"That's right."

"What do you really think of those two?"

I thought about it. "I'd hire them again should the occasion arise, which it won't."

Vullo went back to work on his fingernails again. After a moment or two he stopped gnawing at them, looked up at me, and said, "I'll make you a proposition."

I nodded. There was no reason to say anything.

"Two weeks," he said. "That's all. I want you to spend two weeks on Arch Mix and then come up with a report on why you think he disappeared. Not why he disappeared, but why *you* think he did." Vullo came down hard on the you. He was watching me carefully to see how I was taking it. I tried to have no expression at all.

"For your two weeks' work," he went on, "I'll pay you—" He paused. I decided that he was something of an actor. "Ten thousand dollars."

I had always wondered what my price was. Apparently it was ten thousand dollars for two weeks' work because I said, "All right," and then started planning how Ruth and I were going to spend quite a bit of money in Dubrovnik. I had heard that it's really quite pleasant there in the fall.

4

Vullo called both Murfin and Quane into his office, told them about the arrangement he had made with me, and instructed them to lend whatever assistance I might require. When Vullo mentioned the amount of money that I was to be paid for my fortnight's effort, Murfin's mouth abruptly went down at the corners in a look of frank appreciation. It sounded as if I'd pulled off something slippery and that made Murfin admire it.

I suggested rather politely, I thought, that Vullo call in a secretary and dictate a letter of understanding, which would, I pointed out, be mutually beneficial.

"He means he wants it in writing," Quane said.

Vullo frowned, thought about it, chewed on a fingernail, and then rang for a secretary. When she came in he dictated the letter rapidly and didn't object at all when I suggested a couple of phrases that I thought might be nice.

"You'll want to wait for it, I suppose," Vullo said.

I nodded and smiled. "Well, you know what the mails are."

"Then perhaps you wouldn't mind waiting in Murfin's office. He'll give you a copy of our file on Mix."

With that Vullo picked up some papers on his desk and lost himself in them. I was dismissed. I was not only dismissed, but I also seemed to have been forgotten.

34

Murfin grinned, shrugged, and jerked his head towards the door. I rose and followed him and Quane out and down the hall into Murfin's office where he handed me a large manila envelope.

"That's our stuff on Mix," he said. "How'd you and Vullo get along?"

"Okay," I said. "He seems a little remote. But he's probably just shy."

"He doesn't believe in what he calls unnecessary social pleasantries," Quane said. "He thinks they're a waste of time. So he's eliminated hello, good-bye, please, thank you and a lot of other stuff like that from his vocabulary. It must save him a couple of minutes a year. Maybe even more."

Murfin grinned again. It was his nastiest one yet. "Who does he remind you of?"

I thought for a moment. "Mix," I said finally. "In a curious kind of way he reminds me very much of Arch Mix."

"Yeah," Murfin said. "That's what I thought you'd say."

*   *   *

The house was on one of the more fashionable stretches of N Street in Georgetown and I had to go around the block three times before I could find a place to park. It was a fairly narrow three-storey house of old red brick. But the brick was just about all that was still old because the front door, the windows, and the wood trim were quite new, although they had been custom made so that they would look just as old as the brick. All that had cost a lot of money, but then the owner of the house had a lot of money.

I walked up the six metal steps to the door and rang the bell. After perhaps a minute or so the door opened slowly. The young woman who stood there was nude, or stark naked, if you prefer, and she said, "Well, Squire, come on in."

I went in and said, "Put some clothes on."

"The air conditioning's on the blink."

"Put some clothes on and sweat a little."

"Jesus, you're such a prude."

She picked up an almost transparent green robe that had been flung over a chair and slipped into it. The robe helped some, but not much, because I could see right through it. But it did nothing for me because the woman's name was Audrey Dunlap, she was thirty-two, a widow, and also my sister, the millionaire dope fiend.

I tried heroin once when I was sixteen and I liked it very much. So much, in fact, that I never tried it again on the theory that anything that made you feel that good must be bad for you. I think I acquired that particular mind set from the German side of my family. Certainly not the French.

Over the years I had tried most of the other drugs out of mild curiosity and most of them only made me feel dopey. Pot does absolutely nothing for me except make me cough a lot and giggle a bit. I never tried LSD, primarily because of my schizoid tendencies which, I have been assured, are pronounced. For my nerves I sometimes take a little gin.

My sister, on the other hand, had never tried heroin because she said she was saving it. I never asked her for what because she might have come up with the answer. She made do, or did the last time I had talked to her, with a little coke and hash and Quaalude and pot, which were all rather fashionable that year and my sister, if nothing else, was fashionable.

"Well," she said, "I suppose you want a drink."

"You got anything to eat?"

"You know where it is."

"Where's Sally?" I said. Sally Raines was my sister's black companion, confidante, social secretary, and connection.

"She took the kids over to the park."

"How old are they?"

"Six and five," she said. "Do you remember when I was six?"

"Too well."

"Well, they're both just like me."

"A pain in the ass."

"Right."

"Why don't you all come out to the farm Saturday," I said. "I fixed up a swing that goes out over the pond."

"Like the one in Opelousas?"

I looked at her. She was smiling at me. "I didn't think you remembered that," I said.

"I remember everything," she said. "It was the summer of forty-eight. You were fifteen and I was five and the swing went out over the river or the creek or lake or whatever it was and you held me and then we fell a mile into the water. That was a hell of a summer, wasn't it?"

"It was fine," I said. "So why don't you bring the kids out Saturday?"

"Ruth wouldn't mind?"

"You know Ruth."

"Ruth's all right," she said. "The only thing wrong with Ruth is that she makes me feel as if I've got some part missing. By comparison, I mean. I like her. I like her a lot. Did I ever tell you that?"

"You didn't have to."

"But then you and I don't ever talk about anything, do we?"

"Who does?"

"Do you and Ruth?"

"Sometimes."

"What about?"

"Everything," I said. "Anything. Nothing."

"It must be fun."

"It's different."

We were still in the living room, which was furnished in my sister's eclectic but impeccable taste. It was a blend of antique and contemporary furniture although blend makes it sound far too tame. Everything contrasted dramatically without jarring and the living room and the entire house, for that matter, had appeared in the Sunday supplements of half a dozen or so newspapers. Often Audrey, and maybe the kids, too, would be seen in the pictures all dressed up, and even if you knew her very well and looked very closely, you couldn't tell that the beautiful young matron was half spaced out.

I followed her back into the kitchen. "You want something to eat?" I said as I opened the refrigerator, which was large enough to have done for a small hotel.

"I just got up," she said. "I think I'll have some tea."

I turned, put the kettle on, and went back to the refrigerator. There was a lot to choose from—cold roast beef, ham, fried chicken, several kinds of wurst, and maybe nine kinds of cheese. I decided on a chicken leg and roast beef sandwich. My sister watched as I made it.

"Guess who called the other day?" she said.

"Who?"

"Slick."

The kettle started to whistle so I put a tea bag in a cup, poured the water in, and placed the saucer on top of the cup on the unproved theory that it would make it steep better. Then I went back to the refrigerator and took out a can of beer. It was Coors beer. It would be.

"Well," I said. "How's Slick?"

"Chipper," she said. "Jaunty. Maybe even ebullient."

"And as full of shit as ever."

"I don't know," she said. "I only talked to him over the phone. He asked about you."

"What'd he ask?" I said, moving my sandwich and beer over to the kitchen table, which provided a view of the garden, fountain and all. The garden also had been featured in the Sunday supplements. My sister sat down opposite me with her tea.

"He wanted to know if you were still in hiding."

"What'd you tell him?"

"That as far as I knew you still were."

I shook my head. "I'm not in hiding. We've got a phone in and everything now. You've got the number. So does Slick."

"Does it ever ring?"

"Last week," I said. "It rang last week."

"Did you answer it?"

"I was outside and by the time I got there they'd hung up."

"Have you got a cigarette?" she said.

"I'll roll you one."

"God, you're quaint." She rose, found a carton in a cabinet, tore open a pack, and lit the long, brown cigarette with a paper match. She blew some smoke out and said, "That suit. Are you supposed to be dressed up or something?"

I looked down at my suit. "What's wrong with it?"

"It's ten years old. At least ten."

"Eleven."

"What's the occasion?" she said. "The last time you dropped by you were wearing your Big Mack overalls and your shit-kicker high-tops."

"Somebody wants to pay me a whole bunch of money for two weeks' work. I thought I should look neat and earnest."

"I liked the overalls better. Who's paying you the bunch of money?"

"Roger Vullo."

Audrey made a face indicating that she didn't think much of Roger Vullo.

"You know him?" I said.

"We've met. He's weird. What're you supposed to do for him?"

"Give him my opinion about what happened to Arch Mix."

She took it well enough. There was a slight tremor in her left hand as she raised the cigarette to her lips, but I wouldn't have seen it if I hadn't been looking for it.

"You're a real son of a bitch, aren't you?" she said.

"Probably."

She got up and went over to the sink and ran the burning end of her cigarette under the tap and dropped it down the disposal. She switched on the disposal and let it run for a while, for much longer than was really needed. Then she turned back.

"It's funny," she said.

"What?"

"How much alike you and Slick are."

"Sure."

"When Slick called last week he wanted to know all about the kids and me. He must have talked for fifteen minutes about that. I thought he'd never shut up. He even offered to take the kids to the zoo. I told him they hated the zoo. Well, he dropped the kids and switched to me. How was I feeling? Was there anything he could do for me? Maybe we could go to dinner soon. And then—ever so casually, he even lapsed into French—he said, by the way, he was just wondering whether I had any idea of what might have happened to Arch Mix. And that was going to be your next question, too, wasn't it, Harvey?''

"Sure," I said again.

"Well, I'll tell you the same thing I told Slick before I hung up on him. I don't know what happened to Arch. We broke up six weeks ago. He vanished or disappeared or dropped out of sight four weeks ago. He's dead by now, I guess. He must be dead.''

"It lasted quite a while, didn't it?"

Audrey turned and started opening and closing cabinets. She finally found what she was looking for, a bottle of Scotch. She poured some into a glass, drank it down, and made a face. She seldom drank. She poured more Scotch into the glass, added water this time, and sat back down at the kitchen table across from me.

"You know how long it lasted," she said. "A year. Then when he broke it off I came running to my big brother for what—solace? Comfort? A pat on the head? Well, I suppose I got as much from you as you've got to give. But Ruth made it worth the trip. She let me talk.''

"I let you talk."

"You let me talk for fifteen minutes and then started fidgeting."

"I made a mistake," I said. "I didn't know how serious it was. Mix wasn't the first married man you'd busted up with.''

"I keep forgetting that I'm the whore of the eastern seaboard.''

"I said I made a mistake. A bad one.''

"I reckon that's as close to an apology as you're capable of," she said. Sometimes my sister used reckon, sometimes guess. The reckon came from the South and the guess came from the North. Her voice was much like our mother's which had had a French tinkle to it although, unlike our mother, Audrey had no accent except upper-income, undefinable American.

She drank a swallow of her Scotch and water and made another face. "How do you people drink this stuff?"

"Practise," I said. "It helps if you don't start before breakfast."

"They came to see me."

"Who?"

"The cops."

"How were the cops?" I said.

"Polite. Firm. Thorough. And puzzled, I reckon. Or maybe that's just how they try to appear. I haven't had too much experience with the police."

"What about Mix?"

"What about him?"

"I mean how did he seem the last time you saw him?"

Audrey lit another of her long brown cigarettes. This time it seemed to taste better to her. "Noble," she said. "He was being noble. Sad, noble and nervous."

"You mean about going back to the kids and the little woman?"

She nodded slowly. "It's strange how some men get after they turn forty or maybe fifty, especially if they marry early. They find something younger and perhaps prettier and they think it's going to be their last chance so they grab it. But then they get guilty or scared or both and go back to where it was safe. Dull, perhaps, but safe."

"You said he was nervous. Was there anything else that was worrying him?"

"If there was he didn't talk about it. We talked about Us and Art and Literature and Life. I tried to capitalize all those things, but I'm not sure I made it."

"You did all right."

"And sometimes he'd talk about Her. That's capitalized, too."

I nodded.

"Well, one time he said that shortly after he'd turned

forty he woke up, rolled over, and realized that for fifteen years he'd been married to a stranger."

"That's not very noble."

"But think of the sacrifice he made by going back to her."

"She's not all that bad."

"Mother would have said coarse."

"Mother was a snob."

Audrey shrugged. "So am I."

"You can afford to be."

"It's funny, but he was never interested in that. The money, I mean. I can tell. Jesus, how I can tell."

"Well, rich young widows are rather popular."

"He mentioned you a couple of times," she said. "In passing."

"Oh? He spoke well of me, I trust."

"Not very."

"What'd he say?"

"He said you were a man with principles but no purpose and that he felt sorry for you."

"You defended me, of course."

"I said I wasn't too sure about the principles."

5

The black Plymouth sedan was still parked across the street from my sister's house and a few doors down. It had been there when I had driven around the block three times looking for a place to park an hour before. Although it was still there, the man behind the wheel was different.

I crossed the street and moved down the sidewalk until I reached the car's front bumper. Then I stopped, took out my tin box, and started rolling a cigarette. The man inside the car watched me. I nodded at him and smiled. He didn't nod back. He didn't smile either. When the cigarette was rolled I walked around to the driver's side and smiled down at the man. He gave me a bleak look.

"Got a match, mister?" I said, all friendly and country.

"I don't smoke."

I patted my pockets, grinned like a fool, took out some matches, and lit the cigarette. Then I gave the Plymouth the look of a man who knows his automobiles.

"Nice car, a Plymouth," I said. "It's the Fury, ain't it?"

The man nodded, but only once. He was about twenty-eight or twenty-nine with a round, plump face, light blue eyes, not much of a nose, and a mouth that was much too harsh and cruel for the rest of him. His hair was a sandy blond and long enough to lap over his shirt collar.

"Bet it's got the big engine in it though," I said in the

knowing tone of one who can't be easily slickered. "Probably uses a lot of gas."

The man made himself look exasperated.

I looked around carefully and then bent down so that my forearm rested on the door sill. I grew a confidential look on my face. "You wouldn't be a kidnapper, would you?"

"A what?"

"My sister lives in that house right over there," I said and pointed. "In about ten minutes her kids are gonna be comin' home from the park. Now my sister's got a little money so I just thought that if you and your buddy, the one who was sittin' right here about an hour ago, well, I thought that if you all were kidnappers, maybe I'd just better go call the cops."

"Aw shit, fella," the man said, reaching into his shirt pocket, and brought out a folding case and let me look at a badge and the ID card that went with it.

"Don't reckon you'd mind, would you?" I said and reached for the case. The ID card said that he was a detective with the Metropolitan Police Department and that his names was James Knaster. It also said he was thirty years old. I studied the card and then handed the case back.

I gave him a huge wink. "Keepin' an eye on her, huh?"

"What's your name, friend?"

"Longmire. Harvey A. Longmire."

"Why don't you just run along, Mr. Longmire?"

"You vice?" I said and before he could reply I went on with my rube act, which even Ruth says isn't bad. "You know what she's doing, don'tcha? She's sittin' up there in a fancy wrapper you can see right through drinkin' Scotch whiskey and hit not yet noon."

"Look, fella—"

"Reckon the best thing I can do is go tell her that you're out here keepin' an eye on her sinnin' ways. Dear Lord, I'm just so glad our old Mom and Daddy ain't alive to see this." I shook my head sorrowfully and patted the sill of the car door. "Well, Detective Knaster, it sure has been pure inspiration just talkin' to you."

I turned and started back towards Audrey's house. Behind

me I could hear the Plymouth's engine start. I looked back as Knaster pulled the car out from the kerb and drove off. He didn't look at me. I waved anyhow.

*   *   *

Like Georgetown, Washington's Foggy Bottom was once a slum. A black slum. But now it's home for the State Department and there isn't much fog to speak of, although there are those who will argue that it has increased markedly since the State Department settled in.

What's left of the Foggy Bottom residential area is still rather fashionable, and therefore expensive, and Jean-Jacques Le Gouis, my Uncle Slick, wouldn't have dreamed of living in any other kind of neighbourhood. Home to him was a small house on Queen Anne's Lane where it was even more difficult to park than in Georgetown. However, I found an empty slot after only fifteen minutes and perhaps two quarts of gasoline. Taking the gasoline into consideration, I estimated that the free parking space had saved me approximately thirty-five cents. Somehow I resisted the temptation to jot it down.

The house was a narrow, two-storey, flat-front frame building painted a light pastel blue with cream trim. The front yard was about the size of your average living room rug and a lot of painstaking care had been spent on turning it into a Japanese garden. There was even a little pool with a little bridge that had a little stone troll on guard. The troll looked faintly Asiatic. I had been assured that the garden was quite authentic, but I could only think of it as precious. I refused to think of it as cute. After all, he was my uncle.

I rang the bell twice and while I waited I admired the thick old wooden door that had been cut down from one that once had provided entrance into a century-old Presbyterian church that had been razed to make way for a McDonald's. My uncle was always scouting demolition sites for fine old wood, stained glass, marble, and other interesting doodads that he somehow incorporated with his decorating scheme that included an all-marble bathroom with a huge stained glass window depicting Moses in the bullrushes.

I was about to ring again when I heard his voice ask, "Who is it?" He didn't open the door to just anyone. Not many people in Washington do, other than my sister. But Slick had grown especially wary since the time he reluctantly had opened it to a soft-spoken young couple who claimed to be Jehovah's Witnesses. They had promptly bopped him over the head and made off with about $2,000 in cash and valuables.

When he said, "Who is it?" again I replied. "It's your poor nephew, Uncle. Come to seek a boon."

He opened the door then. "Well, dear boy."

"I'm forty-three, Slick."

"Almost a child. I'm fifty-six."

"You don't look it."

"Don't lie to an old man, Harvey."

I wasn't really. He still had all of his hair and it was thick and glossy and black on top and silver at the sides. He had kept his weight down and there wasn't much sag to his lean face that had some interesting lines that a stranger might have taken for character. It was, all in all, a handsome, faintly hawkish face that easily could have passed for fifty or maybe even forty-nine and if I hadn't known that he couldn't see three feet in front of him, I would never have suspected that his green eyes were covered by contacts.

My uncle's living room was furnished with antiques that he had collected over the years so I sat down gingerly on a couch that looked to be the sturdiest of the lot.

"Have you had lunch?" he asked.

"Audrey fed me."

"Well. How is Audrey?"

"All right."

"I was about to have a martini, but since you've eaten perhaps you'd like something else."

"A beer would be fine."

My uncle nodded, went through the dining room into the kitchen, and came back with a tray that bore a tall Pilsener glass, a bottle of imported Beck's beer, another glass, and a small silver shaker that I presumed contained his martini. He put the tray down, poured my beer, gave the shaker a couple of swirls, filled his glass, and carefully sipped his drink.

The final part of his ritual was a solemn, judicious nod and after he was through with that I said, "What do you care what happened to Arch Mix?"

"I like your moustache. Is it new?"

"It's two years old."

"It makes you look faintly like Fredric March. A young Fredric March, of course."

"Come on, Slick."

He reached inside his blue blazer, brought out a silver cigarette case, politely offered me one, which I refused, took one for himself, lit it, and then smiled and said, "Audrey told you of my interest, of course."

"That's right."

"Well, you might say I have a professional interest in what happened to Arch Mix."

"I thought you'd retired."

"From the agency, dear boy, but not from life. I started up my own little consultancy about a year ago. Yes, I suppose you wouldn't know about that because we haven't seen each other in almost two years, isn't it?"

"About that."

"I got your Christmas card. Did you get mine? Yours was really quite clever."

"Ruth did it."

"How is that charming woman?"

"Fine."

"Remarkable woman."

"Yes."

"However does she stand the isolation?"

"She has me."

"Yes, she does have you, doesn't she, and the goats, too, of course." He made it sound as if the goats were her salvation.

"Let's get back to Mix," I said.

"Well, dear boy, I suppose I really should ask why you

would even care that I'm interested in what happened to Mr. Mix."

"Roger Vullo is going to pay me a lot of money to tell him what I think happened."

"Just for your thoughts on the matter?" He had picked up immediately on the think I had used, which was another good reason to call him Slick.

"Just for my thoughts," I said.

"Little Roger," Slick said in a musing, almost dreaming tone. "I knew his daddy quite well, you know."

"I didn't."

"Yes, we served in the OSS together. Little Roger wasn't born then, of course."

"No."

"I understand he has set up a foundation of sorts to look into all kinds of interesting things."

"Conspiracy," I said. "He sees it everywhere."

"Well, they do seem to be burgeoning everywhere."

"Conspiracies?"

"No, dear boy, organizations or foundations or committees or what have you that have been set up to poke about in them. Most of the time they seem to be dead set on casting my former masters as the villain in each piece."

"The agency has always been blameless, of course."

Slick smiled. "I prefer to think of us as having been a bit careless here and there."

"Mix," I said. "Let's get back to him."

"Yes. Let's. Well, after I retired I was really at loose ends so I talked to some old friends who suggested that I might set up my little consultancy. Which I did."

I looked around the living room. "Where?"

"Right here. I fixed up one of the spare bedrooms into quite a nice little office. In fact, I found a rolltop desk in Leesburg that was an absolute steal. My office has rather a charming 1904 air about it."

I drank some of my beer and then took out my tin box and started rolling a cigarette. "Try not to spill any, dear boy," Slick said, "I've just vacuumed."

I didn't spill any. "What do you consult on, Slick?"

"Shall I be modest?"

"Don't even try."

"Well, during my years of service I acquired a certain amount of expertise that a number of old friends seem to think most highly of. They recommend me to firms and organizations and even individuals who are having a spot of trouble."

"Give me an example."

"I'll give you two. They were both cases of industrial espionage. Some Germans were the culprits in one, which concerned pharmaceuticals. The Japanese were mixed up in the other. Electronics. Down in Dallas. It was really rather quite like old times."

"Which pharmaceutical company was it?"

"Well, as a matter of fact, it was Vullo Pharmaceuticals. Something of a coincidence, don't you think?"

"Sure."

"Young Roger, of course, has nothing to do with the company's operations."

"So I understand."

We sat there in silence for a moment, eyeing each other, waiting to see who would be the first to say something inane about the twists of fate. When neither of us did I said, "Who hired you to look into Arch Mix?"

"Well, I wasn't really hired. I was retained."

"Sorry."

"Actually, I've been retained by the union."

I shook my head and I think I kept on shaking it as I said, "I don't believe it. I honestly don't believe it."

"Well, there was never anything to tie me to that other dismal business back in 1964," Slick said. "And besides, I was only on the periphery of it."

"You were in up to your ass."

"My involvement was marginal," he said in his stiffest tone, "and it never became public."

"So how did the union stumble over you?"

"They retained eminent legal counsel. After Mix vanished they felt they should do something so they turned to counsel for advice. Counsel suggested the Pinkertons, but when it was pointed out that the Pinkertons, have rather a spotty labour record, my name came up." He waved a hand. "Mutual friends, you know."

"When did all this happen?"

"Four weeks ago."

"Who's your contact at the union?"

"The vice-president. Warner B. Gallops. A black gentleman. Do you know him?"

"I know him."

"I wonder what the B stands for?"

"Baxter."

"Oh my. Well, he seems quite shrewd. Or perhaps I should say clever."

"He's both."

"How well do you know him?" Slick asked.

"At one time we were friends, but then he decided that he'd rather be friends with Mix than with me so we're not friends any more."

"There's more to it than that, of course."

"He doublecrossed me a long time ago," I said. "But if you asked him about it, he'd probably tell you that I doublecrossed him. It was internal politics. Anyway, it's one of the reasons that Gallops is vice-president of the union."

"An opportunist?"

"Aren't we all."

"I didn't ask, of course, but I obtained a copy of the union's constitution and it provides that the vice-president will serve as president should the incumbent die, be absent, or incapacitated."

"I like the way your mind works, Slick."

"One has to look for motive."

"That's probably why you were hired. Sorry. Retained."

"Oh, quite. Mr. Gallops made that most clear. I think I can remember his exact words. He said, 'You got two jobs, buddy. First, you're gonna find out what happened to Arch and, second, you're gonna prove that I had fuck all to do with it.' " Slick was an excellent mimic.

"So what've you turned up?" I said.

"Virtually nothing."

"And the cops?"

"Less."

"What's the FBI doing?"

"Their usual."

"You have lines into both places, I take it."

"Well, yes, I've cultivated several sources, of course, and then I can always call on a few old friends, if need be."

"Slick?"

"What?"

"Just how many old friends have you got? A rough guess."

He thought about it for a moment, sipped his martini, and then said, "Well, I really don't quite know how to answer that. I send out around eight hundred Christmas cards each year and I receive approximately that many. But they're not all *close* friends, of course."

"Eight hundred?"

"Why, yes. How many do you send?"

"Last year I think we sent around nine."

"Nine hundred?" He was impressed.

"No, just nine cards. We got ten, so we're still ahead."

"They *are* beautiful cards."

"Ruth does each one individually."

"That remarkable woman."

"You said you turned up virtually nothing. What does virtually mean?"

"Well, first, of course, there was the possibility of a kidnapping. The union has scads of money now, you know. Not quite like the old days. But there's been no ransom demand. Then, of course, I totted up Mix's enemies and, I must say, they're absolutely legion. He seems to have a most acerbic personality."

"Any particular enemies? As you say, he has a lot."

My uncle shrugged and finished the last swallow of his martini. "Well, there're at least a dozen governors, fifteen or twenty mayors, and perhaps a couple of dozen city managers to whom he is simply anathema—not to mention a host of county officials. Then, too, there seem to be a couple of hundred dissidents within the union. I'm not talking about the rank and file members, but rather about local and regional officers of varying power and prestige who absolutely loathe him. I don't think loathe is too strong a word.''

"Probably not," I said.

"And then, of course, there's Audrey, the woman scorned."

"When did you find out about them?" I said. "It was supposed to be a secret."

"Dear boy, it was common gossip around town at least six months ago. Certain friends of mine even delighted in giving me regular reports about the affair's progress. It almost got into the papers, in fact, especially after Mix broke it off."

"Well, Audrey isn't much of a one to sneak around."

"No, she isn't. I've often wondered how she ever met him."

"I introduced them," I said.

"*You?*"

It took a lot to surprise or startle Slick, but when I saw that I'd succeeded I smiled. "It was a cocktail party," I said. "One of those fund-raising things that Audrey sometimes gets involved in until she gets bored. I don't even remember what it was for. Something chic and wholesome. Anyway, Ruth was in town to see her dentist and we called Audrey just to say hello and she insisted that we go to the thing."

"Ruth and you at a cocktail party?" Slick shook his head in mild wonder. I was full of surprises that day.

"It was the first one we'd been to in three years. Maybe even more. Arch Mix was there and he came over to me, probably to trade insults, and I introduced him to Audrey who was on her best behaviour. You know, all wit and sex and charm."

Slick nodded. "The woman can be an absolutely fascinating voluptuary when she chooses."

"Have you ever seen Mix's wife?"

He nodded again. "I've talked with her several times."

"I suppose Audrey was on the prowl. She gets like that

occasionally. Well, Mix didn't stand a chance. Not many men would. So that's how it started.''

"And lasted a year?"

"About that."

"And how is Audrey?" he said. "I know I've already asked that, but what I mean is how does she look to you?''

I shrugged. "All right. Somebody seems to have her under surveillance of some kind."

"What do you think it is, drugs or Mix?"

I shook my head. "I don't know. I ran one of them off with a rube act that shouldn't have bothered anyone. He showed me a badge and some ID that said his name was Knaster. James Knaster—with a K. He's supposed to be a detective. About thirty."

Slick stared at me for a moment. Then he picked up the phone, dialled, and asked for Clarence. I couldn't tell whether Clarence was the first name or the last, but when Clarence came on they chatted for a while like old friends and then Slick said, "I was just wondering if you could give me a bit of information about a young chap who works for you people. His name is Knaster—that's with a K. Detective James Knaster." He waited, listened for a while, then thanked Clarence profusely, and hung up.

Slick looked at me and then held up his fingernails and gave them a close examination. While he was still admiring them he said, "They have no one named Knaster. They've never had anyone by that name."

6

Slick and I speculated for a while about why anyone with a fake police ID would want to keep a watch on my sister's house. We ran through several ideas, all of them rather unimaginative, and we seemed to be running out of any ideas at all when the phone rang. Slick answered it, said, "Of course," and then handed it to me. It was Max Quane.

"How'd you know where to find me?" I said.

"I called your wife and she said you might be at your sister's and your sister gave me this number. I told her it was important."

"Well, is it?"

Something had crept into Quane's voice. It made him talk too fast and run some of his words together. "I've got to see you, Harvey," he said.

"Why?"

"I've just got to, damn it."

"All right. When?"

"Right away," Quane said. "Now."

"Well, I suppose I can get down there in fifteen minutes."

"No," he said quickly. "I'm not at the office. I've got a little apartment over on Mintwood Place. You know where Mintwood Place is?"

"Just give me the address," I said.

He gave it to me and, as usual, I had nothing to write

with so I repeated it. It sometimes helps, but not always. Then I said, "Max."

"What?" he said and his voice was so low and indistinct that I had trouble hearing him.

"Just give me a hint, will you? A small one will do."

There was a silence that lasted several seconds. I thought I could hear him breathing harshly and for a moment I was afraid he might be hyper-ventilating. But a phone can play tricks. Finally, he sighed and it was a deep one that seemed to have a sob clinging to its end.

"I—" He started, stopped, and finally when he spoke again it came out in one tumbling rush, the words jamming themselves up against each other.

"I think I know what happened to Arch Mix."

The phone went dead. Apparently Quane had hung up. He had been very mysterious and very dramatic and possibly even very silly, which wasn't at all like him. Over the years, Quane had turned into what I couldn't help thinking of as a rather cool number, what with his vested suits, his tab collars, and his empty grey eyes that seemed to price everything and find it all far too cheap.

I tried to keep what I was thinking, or perhaps feeling, off my face when I turned to Slick and said, "I'll make you a deal."

"What kind of deal?"

"A trade-off."

"Yes," he said and nodded. "I see. You're suggesting more of a pool than a trade-off, aren't you?"

"All right. A pool."

"And what do you propose to drop into our little pool?"

"I've already dropped Knaster. That should be something."

"Possibly, providing Knaster has something to do with Mix as well as Audrey."

"It's all I've got."

"And now it's my turn?"

"Yes."

"Very well, Harvey, what do you need?"

"An appointment with your client?"

"Gallops?"

"Yes."

"When?"

"Today," I said. "The earlier the better."

There was that about Slick. You didn't have to spend the afternoon explaining things to him. He thought for a moment, working up his pitch, I assumed, then picked up the phone, dialled, and after a few more moments got through to Warner B. Gallops. It was a pleasure to listen to Slick sell. First he was charming, then he was winning, and finally he was convincing—especially when he lied, which he did beautifully, particularly about what a valuable contribution I was making to the investigation.

"Well?" I said after he hung up.

"Eleven o'clock tomorrow."

"Not today?"

"No. Not today."

"All right then. Tomorrow. What was that Gallops called me when you first mentioned my name?"

"A shitbird, I believe," Slick said. "After that it got somewhat less complimentary."

* * *

The last I had heard, Max Quane was still living with his wife and two sons out in the Bannockburn section of Bethesda, Maryland, just off Wilson Boulevard not too far from the old Chesapeake and Ohio canal. It was a fairly upper middle-class section whose residents had tended to shun grapes, boycott lettuce, and now worried a great deal about what the Japanese were doing to the whales.

On the other hand, Mintwood Place was a fairly seedy block of row houses just off the Columbia Road back of the Hilton about half a block from Kalorama Park. The block that contained the address that Quane had given me was partly black, partly Cuban, and partly white. If you didn't know where to look it was a street hard to find, hard to get to, and impossible to park near. It was also, I decided, a rather good place for a man to keep a small furnished apartment that was none of his wife's business.

It was nearly two o'clock by the time I found a place to park on Nineteenth Street near Biltmore. I took off my coat, loosened my tie, and walked up Nineteenth to Mintwood where I turned left. It was hot—hot for Washington, hot for New Orleans, hot even for Africa, and by the time I had gone half a block my shirt was damp. By the time I had gone a block it was wet. A couple of small, dark Cubans without shirts sat quietly on a small stoop and shared a bottle of something in a brown paper sack. They watched me carefully as I went by, probably because they had nothing better to do and I was something to look at. Not much, just something.

The address that Quane had given me was a three-storey row house built out of beige brick. It still had a porch and on it two small children, a boy and a girl with solemn Spanish eyes, were trying to screw a lightbulb into an empty wine bottle. They weren't having much luck, but they seemed interested in their problem.

I went through a screen door into a small foyer whose only furnishing was a stolen supermarket cart with a missing wheel. There was a row of six mailboxes with locks, but most of them had been prised open at one time or another. The mailboxes had small spaces for the names of the building's tenants. Four of the spaces were filled in; two weren't. In the space for number six, which supposedly was Quane's, someone had printed in Johnson.

I started up the stairs and didn't meet anyone until I reached the second landing and turned to go up the remaining flight to the third storey. A man came down the stairs. He was in a hurry, maybe even a rush, because he took the steps two at a time. I stepped back out of his way. He didn't see me at first because he was watching his feet, making sure not to trip. He looked up finally, saw me, hesitated—or seemed to—and then kept on going. I thought he even picked up a little speed.

He was a wide, stocky man with short legs. He had heavy black eyebrows and a dark face that could have been tanned, but wasn't. He was about thirty-five. He wore a suit. A light blue one. I turned to get a better look at him because I thought I'd seen those heavy eyebrows somewhere before. But all I got was a glimpse of the back of his head. There was a round, white bald spot in his crown about the size of a cookie.

I went on up the stairs on the third floor trying to remember where I had seen the man before. Quane's apartment, number six, seemed to be towards the back, to my right. I started down the hall. It had the smell of sour milk and Spanish spices. When I reached number six I found the door open. Not much. Just an inch or so. I knocked, but when nobody said anything and nothing happened I went in.

The place wasn't much of a love nest. It was merely a kitchen to the right and a bathroom to the left. The furnishings were simple, almost rudimentary. There was a table of Formica and chrome, which I think they still call dinettes, and four matching chairs. It looked fairly new as did the sofa, which was the kind that could be made into a bed. On the floor was a cheap rug. A green one.

There were a couple of other chairs, a lamp or two, and in front of the sofa was a coffee table. On it was a phone, the black push-button kind. Next to the phone was a full cup of black coffee with a saucer and a spoon.

I said, "Max?" and then I said, "Anybody home?"

I was looking towards the kitchen, thinking that Quane perhaps had forgotten the cream or the sugar for his coffee. There was a sound to my left. I looked. Max Quane came out of the bathroom.

He came out slowly, on his hands and knees, crawling, although he looked as if he might just be learning how to crawl; the way a baby learns. He was crawling towards the phone. It was hard. The phone was far away, at least eight feet, perhaps even nine. Quane made a yard, crawling on his hands and knees. Then he stopped crawling and collapsed on the green rug, facing my way, his grey eyes open and staring up at me although I don't think they really saw me. I don't think they saw anything.

Ear to ear. That's how throats are cut. "His throat was cut from ear to ear." I had read it many times, but I couldn't remember where. Max Quane's throat had been cut, but whoever had done it must not have been much of a reader, because he hadn't bothered about ear to ear. There was a deep, short slash on each side of Quane's throat. The slashes had reached the big arteries. There was a lot of blood on Quane, and he had left a trail of it on the green rug as he had tried to learn how to crawl all over again and had made a yard before he had quit trying and died.

The rest of the blood must have been in the bathroom and I remember thinking that it would be easier to clean up there. It wasn't much of a thought, but I wasn't thinking too clearly. I stood there, not moving, staring down at Quane. He stared back up at me, or seemed to, but his eyes didn't move and they didn't blink and after a moment or so I knelt down and felt for his pulse, but I didn't find any. I hadn't really expected to.

I rose and went into the kitchen. There was nobody there. Just a kettle and a jar of Yuban instant coffee and a box of sugar cubes. I felt the kettle. It was warm, nearly hot. I made myself go look into the bathroom. There are five quarts of blood in the human body, but there seemed to be more than that in the bathroom. It was all over everything, the tub, the toilet, the sink, the floor, even the walls.

Bathrooms are where you go when you're going to be sick. But I couldn't go in there so I hurried back into the kitchen and threw up in the sink. After that I ran some cold water and washed my face and dried it with a paper towel.

I went back into the living room, skirting Max Quane, trying not to look at him, but not succeeding. I moved towards the phone that rested on the coffee table next to the cup and the saucer and the spoon. I was going to use the phone to call the police and tell them that Max Quane was dead.

It was then that I really saw the spoon. I stared at it, picked it up and looked at it closely. I must have looked at it for almost half a minute. It made me remember many things and wonder about even more. I put the spoon in my pocket.

I then turned to leave the apartment where Max Quane lay dead with his throat cut. I was going to leave without either calling the police or looking at Quane again. I didn't call the police, but I couldn't help but look at Quane. Although they didn't want to, my eyes went to his throat where the slashes were. Below the slashes was his tab collar with its neat little gold pin. There didn't seem to be any blood on the pin.

7

I don't know why I went through Georgetown. I didn't even remember getting there. But when I realized where I was I pulled into a gas station on M Street and used a pay phone to call the police. I told whoever answered that they could find a murdered man in the apartment on Mintwood Place. I didn't say who the murdered man was, I didn't say who I was, but I did say that the dead man's throat had been cut and then I made myself hang up because I had the feeling that if I didn't, I would add that the dead man's throat had been cut from ear to ear and that wasn't at all the way it had happened.

It got a little better after that. But only a little. I remembered that there was something I had to do. I couldn't quite recall what it was until I was almost to Key Bridge and then I remembered that Ruth had told me that we needed some gin. Well, that was true. We did need some. Quite a lot, in fact, so I stopped in a liquor store and bought two fifths of Gilbey's. Or perhaps it was Gordon's. I really don't remember.

I do remember getting one of the bottles open and taking my first gulp before I was halfway across Key Bridge. I gagged on the straight warm gin, but it stayed down, and after a few minutes it did what it was supposed to do to my nerves because my foot no longer twitched on the accelerator.

It wasn't until I'd had my second gulp of gin that I realized that I was going the long way—out the George Washington Parkway to the 495 beltway and then west on Leesburg Pike to Leesburg where I would pick up Route 9 to Harpers Ferry. It wasn't really the long way in miles, but it was the long way in time. The quicker way was to use 1270 to US 340 and then head south. That was longer, but quicker.

I took out my tin box and rolled three cigarettes with one hand because I knew I'd smoke at least that many before I got home and probably more. I had to roll the windows up so that the tobacco wouldn't blow around and by the time I'd finished rolling the cigarettes it was stifling in the pickup and I was sweating all over. I imagined that I could feel the gin oozing from my pores. I lit one of the cigarettes, rolled the windows down, and had another drink.

Although I may have thought that it could, the gin didn't keep me from thinking about Max Quane. All that it really did was make me sweat and stop the twitching in my foot. The right one.

I thought about Quane and his throat and how it had been cut and again I found myself resisting the phrase ear to ear. I wondered when it had happened and decided that it must have happened while I was passing the two bare-chested Cubans who were sharing a bottle of something out of their brown paper sack. That meant it had happened about a minute or two before I got to the three-storey row house and passed the two children on the porch and started up the stairs where I had met the wide man with the short legs and the thick dark eyebrows whom I had seen somewhere before, but couldn't remember where.

It was easy to remember where I had first met Max Quane. It had been twelve years before when he had been only a few years out of some Colorado college with a degree in something useful such as psychology. He had gone to work for the Public Employees Union in Denver as an organizer and because he was quick and smart they had brought him to Washington and by the time I met him he was what was called an International Representative.

Ward Murfin was then the union's director of organization although he had been only twenty-seven at the time. Stacey Hundermark, the soft, gentle president of the Public Employees Union, had felt in probably an uncomfortable sort of way that he needed someone he could trust on his side who was hard and mean and that's why he had made Murfin director of organization. At twenty-seven Murfin was as hard and as mean as they come.

Murfin and Quane had made a team of sorts after that and I remembered that I had hired them as such during four separate political campaigns that I had been called in on between 1966 and 1972. Over all those years Ward Murfin didn't change much. He just stayed hard and mean although his lust for details might have grown a little.

Quane changed. He remained as quick and as smart as always, but as his illusions went he found nothing to take their place, not even ambition, because to be ambitious you had to believe that it all really meant something, and Quane knew better than that.

So he went after money, because it at least always added up the same way, and he wasn't too particular about how he got his hands on it. When he wasn't working with Murfin, Quane was quite often involved in some get rich quick scheme that sounded suspicious and usually was much worse than that. But sometimes the schemes paid off and for a time Quane would have a bundle of cash that he spent quickly in a determined, joyless, almost grim sort of way.

But most of his schemes were like the Mexican dope deal that had involved the old World War II Air Corps pilot. I wondered if Quane had been mixed up in something like that with the wide, short-legged man with the heavy eyebrows who had come hurtling down the stairs. But that seemed unlikely because I still knew I had seen the short-legged man somewhere before. I just couldn't remember where. Or even when.

So I went over the entire day again, hour by hour, trying to remember everything and everybody. It had been a busy day and by the time I reached Leesburg my recollection of events had me just arriving at Quane's apartment.

Although I really didn't want to I recalled that bloody scene again, everything, even down to the spoon that I had picked up and put in my pocket. I felt my pocket to see whether the spoon was still there. It was and as I touched it I suddenly remembered where I had seen the man with the thick eyebrows and the short legs.

He had been sitting in the black Plymouth sedan when I had first gone into my sister's house in Georgetown. When I had come out of her house he had been replaced by the man who claimed to be Detective Knaster. I remembered the short-legged man not only because of his black caterpillar eyebrows, but also because of the spoon, which reminded me of my sister. I touched the spoon again. I could think about it and what it meant now, or I could think about it tomorrow. I chose tomorrow. I often do when it involves something unpleasant.

When I got home the dogs were glad to see me and so were the cats. The peacocks and the ducks didn't care whether I came home or not. I had named all of the dogs Old Blue, regardless of their colour, breed, and size. They didn't seem to mind. The cats, with the exception of Honest Tuan, the Siamese, were all called Fluff. They didn't seem to mind either. They didn't even mind when I called them kitty, which is what I usually did.

It was nearly four by the time I got home and Ruth was on the porch by the pond drinking a glass of ice tea. When I leaned down and kissed her she smiled and said, "You reek of gin, sir."

"Probably."

"Are you drunk?"

"No, but I'm thinking about it."

She looked at me carefully. "Bad?" she said.

I nodded. "Very bad."

"Sit down and I'll get you something to help you get drunk."

I sat down and she went into the house and came back with a tall gin and tonic. I rolled a cigarette, lit it, took a sip of the drink, and stared out over the pond at the farm.

It wasn't really a proper farm, of course, because most of

it ran straight up the mountain. Old man Pasjk, who had sold me the place, claimed that his father and brother had made a living from its eighty acres for nearly 100 years, but I found that hard to believe.

The house, which had been built in 1821, was nothing but a rambling shell when I bought it. It doubtless would have been cheaper and far more practical to have torn it down and built a new one. Instead, I had spent a lot of money remodelling it because there had been no plumbing and the electrical system could only be described as a hazard.

So I had put in a septic tank and two bathrooms and a modern electric kitchen and as a result the plumber had been able to send his oldest son to Yale. When the electrician got through, I think he took his wife on a round the world cruise.

I was thinking about the farm because I didn't much want to think about anything else, especially the day I had just gone through, when Ruth said, "You had two telephone calls."

"Who from?"

"One was from Senator Corsing. Or rather it was from his office. The Senator would like you to call him tomorrow."

"Why?"

"The young lady who called didn't say."

"The other call?"

"It was from Mr. Quane. I gave him Audrey's number. Did he reach you?"

"Quane?"

"Yes."

"Quane's dead," I said. "Maybe I'd better tell you about it."

Ruth looked at me gravely and then in an equally grave tone she said, "Yes, perhaps you'd better."

So I told her about it, about the entire day, about everything— except the spoon. I didn't tell her about the spoon because I wasn't sure about that yet. When I was sure about it I would tell her.

When I was through talking it was nearly six-thirty and I

noticed with some surprise that I had finished only half my drink. The ice had melted in it, but it was still cool, so I drank some of it anyway.

Ruth was silent for a moment and then she said, "These things really happen, don't they?"

"Yes," I said. "All the time."

"It seems so senseless."

"Yes."

"What I mean is if Mr. Quane thought he knew what happened to Mr. Mix, why would he call you? Why wouldn't he call the police?"

"I don't know," I said, "unless he was working an angle that might make him some money. Quane was like that sometimes."

"And you think the man who killed Mr. Quane was the same man who was watching your sister's house this morning?"

"Yes, he was one of them. There were two."

"Why would they be watching Audrey's house?"

"I don't know."

"Is it something to do with Mr. Mix?"

"I think it's all tied in with Mix."

"How?"

"I don't know," I said.

She looked at me for a while, rather fondly, I thought, and then she smiled.

"Is something funny?"

"In a curious way."

"What?"

"I really shouldn't be thinking of anything funny now."

"Because of Quane?"

"Yes."

"People make jokes at funerals all the time. They don't mean to, but they can't help themselves."

"A mild form of hysteria?"

"Maybe," I said.

"I always thought of Mr. Quane as such a sad man. He always seemed terribly unhappy."

"He probably was."

"Did he have many friends?"

I thought about that for a moment. "No," I said, "I don't think so. He had Murfin. Murfin was his friend. And me. I suppose I was his friend. That's about all. He knew a lot of people, but I think he was a little short on friends."

"Some people need a lot of friends," Ruth said.

"Does all this talk about friends have something to do with what you thought was funny?"

"Perhaps," she said. "I was thinking that it was a little something like a western."

"A western what?"

"Film."

"Oh," I said. "How?"

"When we moved out here four years ago it was because we had our reasons, wasn't it?"

"Yes."

"I was thinking that those reasons were very much like those of the gunfighter in a western who stops gunfighting and settles down to something else."

"Because he's scared?"

She shook her head. "No, because he's tired of being a gunfighter or bored with it or even both."

"God, you're a romantic."

"I'm not through, either," she said. "So he's tending his pea patch or raising his cattle or doing whatever it is that he's decided is better than gunfighting when they come to see him."

"Who?"

"The town folk."

"Ah."

"They're worried."

"About the crooked sheriff."

"Who dominates the town by fear and force."

"And a fast gun."

"One of the fastest," she said.

"Maybe even faster than the old, retired gunfighter."

"Perhaps. Perhaps not. But the town folk turn to him and beg him to do something about the crooked sheriff."

"Do they offer him any money?" I said. "That's not a bad incentive."

"Perhaps they do, but not much, and it's not really the reason that he agrees to help them."

"What's the real reason?"

"He's curious about whether he's still better at what he once did than anyone else."

"He can get killed finding out."

"Not in a western," she said and all the lightness went out of her voice.

There was a pause and then I said, "I think you're trying to tell me something in that elliptical way that you sometimes use. I think you're trying to tell me that you'd prefer me to stay home and tend the pea patch."

"Of course I would," she said. "But there was also something else."

"What?"

"I was also trying to tell you that I understand why you won't."

I rose and went over to her and put my hand on her shoulder. She reached up and put her hand on mine, but she didn't look up at me. She stared out over the pond where the ducks seemed to be holding their evening regatta.

"Well, if it's to be done," I said as gravely as I could, "I think it should be done quickly."

"Yes," Ruth said and gave my hand a squeeze, "but you'd better change your clothes first."

So I changed my clothes and went out and milked the goats. They seemed fairly glad to see me.

8

The next morning at nine I was back in Georgetown knocking on my sister's door. She wasn't naked this time when she opened it. She was wearing white pants, a blue silk blouse, and a scarf on her head. She was also carrying a broom in one hand.

"Jesus," I said, "you look the way TV commercials think a housewife should look."

"Fuck off," she said.

I went in and my niece and nephew bounded into the room with my nephew yelling, "Harvey, Harvey, Mama says we're gonna go out and see you and Ruth Saturday and you got a new swing and everything." Maybe it wasn't a yell, but it was loud.

Before I could reply, Audrey said, "*En français*, goddamn it! *En français*."

My nephew, whose name was Nelson, aged six, frowned, thought about it, and said, "French is too damned hard."

My niece, Elizabeth, age five and a vixen, smiled smugly, and said in rapid, perfect French, "Good day, uncle, I hope you are well and that Aunt Ruth is well and that the dogs and the cats and the ducks and the goats are also well." Then she stuck her tongue out at her brother.

I picked Elizabeth up before her brother smacked her one

and said in French, "The goats asked only yesterday if you were coming Saturday."

"Goats can't talk," her brother said. But he also said it in French. "Goats can only say baaaaaa." That was in French, too, perhaps even the baaaaaa.

"Did you ever speak French to a goat?" I asked him, still in French.

He looked at me suspiciously, but finally gave in with a wary, "No."

"Well, goats speak only perfect French," I said. "So until you're perfect, they won't talk to you."

He still wasn't convinced, but when I put his sister down, he took her hand and said in French, "Let's go outside and play."

My niece turned to me, smiled silkily, and showed off her perfect accent again. "Farewell, uncle, I will enjoy seeing you and Aunt Ruth and the dogs and the cats and the ducks and the goats on Saturday."

"You forgot the peacocks," I said and repeated "peacocks" in English.

That was a new word for her so she pronounced it carefully a couple of times and then said, "And, of course, the peacocks."

Her brother gave her hand a yank and they raced out of the room towards the rear of the house and the garden.

"You're right," I said to Audrey. "They're six and five."

She shook her head. "I think I started them on the French too late. I should have started them at two or three instead of four."

"They're doing fine," I said.

She nodded towards the rear of the house. "Let's go back in the kitchen," she said. "I've got to sweep up the cornflakes. The maid couldn't make it this morning."

"Where's Sally?" I said.

"She's not here either," Audrey said.

Back in the kitchen she poured me a cup of coffee which I drank while I sat at the table and watched her sweep up some spilled cornflakes. I thought she was a little out of practice, but I didn't say anything. When she was done she joined me at the table with a cup of tea.

"Well, you're certainly doing the elder brother role this week," she said. "Two days in a row."

"I was sort of in the neighbourhood."

"You were. Sort of."

"You've decided to come out Saturday then?" I said. "Ruth was tickled when I told her you might."

"Harvey."

"What?"

"What the fuck's on your mind?"

I sighed and took the spoon out of my pocket and put it on the table. Audrey looked at it, picked it up, then stared at me, and said, "Where'd you get this?"

"You recognize it?"

"Christ, yes, I recognize it. It's Mother's."

"You're sure?"

"Of course I'm sure. Good God, you must know what it is. It's what we used on Sunday and Christmas and Thanksgiving and Easter. It's a spoon from the good silver. Mother's good silver. It's even got the L on it. See."

I had already seen the L for Longmire, but I looked anyway.

"You took the silver, didn't you, I mean after Mother died?"

"Sure I took it," she said. "You don't throw silver away. You didn't want it, did you?"

"No, I didn't want it. You still have it, don't you?"

"Of course I still have it."

"Where?"

Audrey thought for a moment. Then she got up and started opening some of the lower drawers in the kitchen cabinets. "Here," she said with a small note of triumph. "I remember that I asked Sally to ask the maid to polish it a couple of months ago. What do you want me to do, count the spoons?"

"That's right," I said. "I want you to count the spoons."

She counted them. "There's supposed to be twelve, but there're only ten."

"What about the forks," I said. "Not the salad forks, just the regular ones."

After she counted them, she said, "Two missing."

"Maybe you'd better count the knives, too."

She looked up at me after she was done. "Two missing. Anything else?"

"No," I said. "They probably wouldn't need anything else."

"Who?"

I took out my tin box and started to roll a cigarette. "Oh, for God's sake!" Audrey said, reached in a drawer, and tossed me a pack of Luckys. "I bought these yesterday after you left. I swore I wasn't going to watch you go through that *macho* cigarette-rolling act of yours again even if I had to buy you a year's supply."

"I didn't know I was being *macho*," I said.

"What else would you call it?"

"Economical."

"Cheap, too."

I put my tin box back, opened the Luckys, and lit one. Audrey was angry, or at least pretending to be. She flounced down into the chair opposite me, providing that one can flounce in pants and a shirt. I decided that she could.

"Okay, Harvey, who's been dipping into the family spoons?"

"What do you think about Max Quane?" I said. Even though she was my sister I watched her closely for a reaction. I also think I hated myself a little.

She had no reaction. She said, "What should I think about him?"

"Didn't you know he was dead?"

"How should I know he was dead?"

"It was in the paper. On TV."

"Harvey."

"What?"

"I haven't read a newspaper in two years. Not the front page anyhow. Sometimes I look at the Style section in the *Post*, but lately I haven't even been doing that. I haven't looked at a TV set in six months—unless you count Captain

Kangaroo or whatever the hell it's called that the kids sometimes look at.''

"You didn't know Max?''

"No, I didn't know Max, if that's what you call him. I know that there was a Max Quane who called up here yesterday for you. He said it was important and he sounded kind of twitchy so I gave him Slick's number. Did he reach you there?''

"Yes.''

"Well, what's all this got to do with Mother's silver?''

I picked up the spoon and looked at it. It was as familiar as an old photograph. "I found this spoon in Max Quane's apartment yesterday after I found him with his throat cut.''

"Jesus!''

"You didn't know him?''

"I already told you I didn't know him.''

"No,'' I said. "You wouldn't know Max. Not that way.''

"You mean I wouldn't be interested in playing house with him and even bringing along my own spoons.''

"It's not your style,'' I said, rose, went over to the coffee pot, and poured myself another cup. "Where's the sugar?''

"In the sugar bowl.''

I found it, put a spoonful in my coffee, stirred it, and said, "Sally still lives here, doesn't she?''

"Sally's family,'' my sister said. "She still has her own place on the third floor, the one we fixed up like a little apartment.''

"But she's not here today?''

"No.''

"Why?''

My sister sighed. "Sally and Quane, huh?''

I nodded. "It looks that way.''

"She got a phone call about eight last night. It made her upset and she told me that she had to go out. I didn't ask why.''

"Are you and she still as close as ever?''

Audrey nodded. "Maybe even more so. I think she saved my life after Jack died.'' Jack Dunlap, Audrey's late husband, had been one of those financial geniuses that Texas sometimes produces. By the time he was thirty he was already a millionaire. At thirty-five, which was when he had married Audrey, he was a millionaire many times over as well as part owner of a professional football team, a power in the Democratic party, a member of the boards of at least a dozen major corporations, and a nut about sports and hunting. In 1972 he had been hunting split-tail grouse in North Dakota. He had climbed over a barbed-wire fence, his shotgun had gone off, and that had been the end of Jack Dunlap. I thought my nephew looked exactly like him. My niece was the image of her mother, which was just as well because Jack had been kind of ugly.

"She's been with you how long?" I said.

"Six years, ever since Nelson was born. I hired her as a social secretary because Jack insisted that I needed one. When I asked him what a social secretary did, he said he didn't know but he had read about them in books. So I hired Sally. She was just out of Smith where she'd gone on a full scholarship and graduated with top honours, which isn't bad for a kid from this town who was born near Ninth and U."

"No," I said, "not bad at all."

Audrey was silent for a moment, as though thinking. "Four weeks ago," she said. "It must have started about four weeks ago."

"Sally and Quane?"

Audrey nodded. "It was a couple of weeks after I'd broken up with Arch—or he had broken off with me, which is actually how it happened. I was pretty upset and Sally came to the rescue again. She urged me to talk about it. And I did."

"How'd you know about her and Quane?"

"I didn't know it was Quane. I just knew it was some-body. She'd leave at odd times. Matinees, I reckon. I asked her about it once or twice, but all she'd say was that he was white and married and that she knew she was a goddamned fool, but that she'd rather talk about my being a goddamned fool than about her being one. So we talked about Arch Mix and me."

I had been up since six and had eaten breakfast at

six-thirty and I was hungry again. I got up and started opening cabinet doors. "Where's the bread?" I said.

"In the bread box," Audrey said.

I found it and dropped two slices into the toaster. "You want some toast?"

"No."

I waited for the toast to pop up, found the butter and some strawberry jam in the refrigerator, put some on the toast, and sat back down at the table. "Did you and Arch ever talk about the union?" I said and took a bite of the toast.

"Sure. We talked about everything. I told you that."

"Just before you split up, was there anything about the union that was bothering him? I mean anything out of the ordinary?"

Audrey looked at me strangely. "He talked about you a lot. It wasn't about you exactly, but it was about you and the union back in sixty-four."

"What did he say?"

She shook her head. "I listened, Harvey, but I didn't keep notes. Maybe I should have because recently Sally's been getting me to talk about the same thing."

"How recently?" I said.

She thought about it. "A month or so. Ever since Arch disappeared."

"What'd she get you to talk about?"

"Well, I wanted to talk about what a rotten, no-good son of a bitch he is but Sally steered it around so that I found myself talking about what he'd told me. Sally's no dummy and I thought she was trying to help me get him out of my system." Audrey looked at me and smiled, but the smile was half sardonic, half rueful. "She was pumping me, wasn't she, for this guy Quane?"

I nodded. "Don't blame her too much. Max was awfully good at manipulating people. It was a speciality of his. One of several."

Audrey looked out the window to where her children were playing in the garden. They were playing tag although Nelson seemed to be bopping his sister a little harder than was really necessary. "I wonder if I told her what your friend Quane wanted to know?"

"You probably told her exactly what he wanted to know."

"How can you be sure?"

"Max called me yesterday. He was, as you said, twitchy, which wasn't at all like Max Quane. He said he had to see me. When I asked him why he said it was because he thought he knew what had happened to Arch Mix."

Audrey rose, went over to a cabinet, took down a canister labelled "pepper," took out a cigarette, and lit it. It wasn't a real cigarette though; it was dope. She drew the smoke down into her lungs, held it, and then let it out slowly.

"Shit," she said. "Does that mean that what I told Sally got Quane killed?"

"Quane got himself killed," I said. "If he'd really figured out what happened to Mix he must have tried to get cute with it. He got cute with the wrong people."

"I wonder what I told her?"

"Was there any single thing that Sally kept coming back to, pressing you on?"

Audrey took another drag on her marijuana, picked up the pepper canister, and sat back down at the table. She offered me the canister but I shook my head.

"Sally's too smooth for that," Audrey said. "I mean she would never make it obvious."

"There must have been something," I said.

Audrey thought about it. "In bed," she said.

"She was interested in you and Mix in bed?"

"Not really. But I once told her that after Arch and I had had a really good fuck he liked to just lie there and think out loud. I didn't mind because I was feeling good and remembering how fine it had been. But it was then that he was relaxed and confident and felt that he could talk about whatever was on his mind."

"So what did he talk about?" I said.

"That's what Sally asked—and kept asking, although I didn't notice it at the time."

"She must have been more specific than that."

"Uh-huh, she was, now that I think about it. She was

especially interested in what Arch talked about just before
we broke up. She kept coming back to that with the excuse
that maybe there was something in what he'd said that
would give me some clue about why it really happened. I
mean our bust-up. So I told her what he'd said as best as I
could remember.''

"But then she would come back for something even more
specific?" I said.

"How do you know?"

"That's how I would have done it," I said.

"You are a shit."

"Come on, Audrey. What the hell did you tell her?"

"She kept coming back to a couple of nights right
towards the last when Arch was talking about you and the
union. He wasn't bad-mouthing you. It was just that he'd
found out something that made him think of you and the
union back in sixty-four.''

"What?"

"I told you I didn't take notes. Anyway, I was half
asleep."

"Just tell me what you told Sally."

"I told her that Arch had told me that they were going to
try to use the union just the way they had used it back in
1964 but that he, by God, was going to put a quick stop to
it. Or something like that."

I slumped back in my chair. "When did you tell her
this?"

"A few days ago. Maybe a week. It was all very casual.
Just talk. Or at least that's the way it seemed then. Does it
mean anything?"

"It sure as hell meant something to Max Quane."

"Does it mean anything to you?"

I thought about Max lying on the cheap green rug with
his throat cut. "I hope not," I said.

9

I used the phone in Audrey's kitchen to make the calls. First I called Senator William Corsing's office. The Senator was in a meeting but had left word that he would very much like to see me at ten o'clock, if that were convenient. If ten wouldn't do, perhaps I could make it at eleven.

The young woman whom I talked to had a voice that sounded the way divinity fudge tastes and when I told her that I could make it at ten her grateful, slightly breathless reply made me feel that maybe with my help the republic could be saved after all.

I called Ward Murfin next and when he came on he didn't say hello, he said, "Max didn't leave any insurance."

"I'm sorry," I said.

Murfin sighed. "Me and Marjorie were up with her most of the night. She kept saying she was gonna kill herself. You know how Dorothy is."

I indeed knew how Dorothy Quane was. Dorothy and I had once had a very brief, incredibly gloomy time twelve years before that in retrospect seemed like one long, wet, dismal Sunday afternoon. I had introduced her to Max Quane and he had won her away from me. I had been grateful to Max ever since. Max had never said whether he was grateful to me for introducing him to Dorothy and I had never asked.

"Well," I said, "what can I do?"

"You can be a pallbearer," Murfin said. "I can't find any fuckin' pallbearers. The guy's thirty-seven years old and I can't find six guys who'll be his pallbearers."

"I don't go to funerals," I said.

"You don't go to funerals," Murfin sounded as if I had told him that I didn't go to bed nights, but hung from the rafters instead.

"I don't go to funerals, wakes, weddings, christenings, church bazaars, political rallies, or office Christmas parties. I'm sorry Max is dead because I liked him. I'll even go by and see Dorothy this afternoon and ask if she and her kids would like to come out and stay at the farm for a while. But I won't be a pallbearer."

"Last night," Murfin said. "They had Max on the six o'clock news last night. Well, Marjorie and me get over there about six-thirty, maybe seven, and Dorothy's already flipped. So hell, you know, we figure we'll stay maybe a couple of hours or so, maybe even three or four, and then we figure the neighbours or somebody else'll come by and take over. Nobody."

"Nobody at all?"

"Just the cops. Nobody came. Nobody even called except some reporters. That's kinda hard to believe, isn't it?"

"Kind of," I said. "Max knew a lot of people."

"You know something?" Murfin said, "I don't think Max had any friends except me. And maybe you, although I'm not too sure about you since you don't wanta be a pallbearer."

I told him again that I'd stop by and see Dorothy that afternoon. Then I asked, "What did Vullo say?"

"Well, he seemed to think that Max went and got himself killed on purpose, you know what I mean? He said he was sorry and all that, but he kinda hurried over it. What he was really interested in was how we were gonna replace Max. I told him I'd work on it and then he wanted to know if I'd heard from you on account of maybe you'd have some ideas."

"I don't have any," I said.

"You tell him that," Murfin said. "He wants to see you today."

"When?"

"This afternoon."

"What time?"

"Two-thirty?"

I thought about it. "I'll come by at two and maybe you and I can figure out what to do about Dorothy."

"Maybe we can figure out how you're gonna tell her who Max was shacked up with."

"Who?"

"A real good-looking black fox, according to the cops."

"Did they tell Dorothy that?"

"Not yet."

"The cops know who she is?"

"She rented the pad under the name of Mary Johnson, but the cops don't figure that's her real name. Paid a hundred and thirty-five dollars for the place, utilities included." Murfin, as always, had savoured the details.

"What *do* the cops figure?"

"They figure that she had a boyfriend or maybe even a husband who found out about her and Max and snuffed him out with a knife. Cut his throat. Did you know that's how it happened?"

"Jesus," I said, not exactly lying.

"I had to go down and identify him last night on account of Dorothy by then was threatening to kill herself for the thirteenth or fourteenth time. You know what?"

"What?"

"Max didn't look too bad," Murfin said. "Not for a guy who'd had his throat cut."

I told Murfin I'd see him at two o'clock and then I called my Uncle Slick and invited him to lunch. But when I told him where and when I wanted to eat he said, "You can't be serious."

"It's family business now, Slick," I said, "and I don't want to talk about it all jammed up against somebody else."

"Well, at least we could have some wine," he said.

I said, "I'll leave that up to you," and hung up.

After that I called a lawyer. It was about time. His name was Earl Inch, I had known him for years, and he was very expensive because he was very good. I had decided that I needed a very good lawyer. When I told him I was in trouble he said, "Good," and we set up an appointment for three-thirty that afternoon. It seemed to be turning into a very long day.

Audrey swung round to face me after I hung up the phone and said, "How much trouble are you in?"

"Just enough so that I need a lawyer. And Slick. He can drop a word here and there that probably won't do any harm."

"You need any money?"

"No, but thanks for asking."

"Sally," she said. "You're going to have to tell the police about Sally, aren't you?"

"Yes."

"Will she be in trouble?"

"I don't see how."

"I wish she'd come home."

"Maybe she will when she gets over the shock."

"Harvey."

"What?"

"If I can do anything, well—you know."

"There's one thing you can do," I said.

"What?"

"Come out to the farm Saturday."

*   *   *

Senator William Corsing's office was in the Dirksen Senate Office Building, which used to be called the New Senate Office Building even though after a while it wasn't very new any more.

The Senator's outer offices suffered from what all Congressional offices suffer from, a lack of space. The staff members were crowded up against each other, fighting for *lebensraum* against files, stacks of documents, boxes of envelopes and stationery, and what seemed to be a monumental pile of old copies of the *Congressional Record*.

But the staff seemed cheerful, busy, and confident that they were doing important work. Perhaps they were. I had to wait only a few minutes before I was shown into the Senator's office by the young woman with the divinity-fudge voice. I think I must have expected something blonde and flighty, but she was a tall, slim, cool-looking brunette about thirty, with smart, even wise brown eyes and a wry smile that let you know that she knew how her voice sounded, but there was nothing she could do about it and, what the hell, sometimes it was useful.

If his staff was cramped for space, the Senator wasn't. He had a large, sunny corner office furnished by the government with leather chairs and a nice big desk. On the walls were photographs of him in the company of people he was proud to know. Most of them were rich and famous and powerful. The others looked as though they were determined to get that way.

There were also some nice photographs of the Ozarks, a shoe factory, the Mississippi River, some farm scenes, and one of Saarinen's 630-foot-high stainless-steel catenary gateway arch which a lot of people in St. Louis still think looks like a plug for McDonald's hamburgers. In addition to the photographs there was a large oil portrait of the Senator in a grave pose that made him look concerned and statesmanlike.

When I first met William Corsing he had been the thirty-year-old boy mayor of St. Louis. That was in 1966. He had very badly wanted to be the boy senator from Missouri, but nobody gave him much of a chance, in fact, almost none at all, and that's why I had been called in. After a rather bitter campaign, nasty even for Missouri politics, he had squeaked in by less than 126 votes after a statewide recount. In 1972 he had run against the Nixon tide and won by fifty thousand votes. He was now forty-two, still young for the Senate, but nobody called him the boy anything any more.

He had put on weight, although not enough to keep him from bounding around his desk to shake hands with me. His hair still flopped down into his eyes and he still brushed it away with a quick, nervous combing gesture. But the hair was no longer light brown, it was grey, and although his lopsided, aw-shucks grin had lost none of its charm, it might have become just a bit more mechanical.

I saw that there were also some new lines in his face, but there should have been at forty-two. His grey eyes, set wide from the beginning of his big, handsome nose, had lost none of their intelligence that bordered on brilliance, and I could feel them running over me in order to assess my own wear and tear. It made me give my moustache a couple of brushes.

"I like it," he said. "It makes you look a little like David Niven—when he was a lot younger, or course."

"Ruth likes it," I said.

"How is she?"

"Still the same."

"Still wonderful, huh?"

"That's right."

"You're lucky."

"I know."

"Sit down, Harvey, sit down, hell, anywhere, and I'll get Jenny to get us some coffee."

I sat down in one of the leather chairs and instead of going around behind his desk and sitting behind it, Corsing sat down in a chair next to me. It was a nice touch, and he knew it was a nice touch, and I didn't mind at all.

Jenny was the tall brunette with the wise eyes and she and the Senator must have used telepathy to communicate, because as soon as we were seated she came into the office bearing a tray with two cups of coffee. "You use one spoonful of sugar, don't you, Mr. Longmire?" she said and gave me another one of her wry smiles.

I looked at Corsing. "Hell," he said and grinned, "that's one you taught me. Always remember what they drink and what they use in their coffee."

As Jenny was serving us the coffee she said, "I understand that you were with the Senator on his first campaign."

"Yes, I was."

"That must have been exciting," she said.

"It was close," I said and smiled.

"Are you handling any campaigns this year?" she said.

"No," I said. "I don't do that any more."

"What a pity," she said, smiled again, and left.

I looked at Corsing again after Jenny had gone. He nodded, sighed not unhappily, and said, "She's the one. Has been for four years now. Smart as hell."

"She seems to be," I said.

"Heard her over the phone?"

"Uh-huh."

"What do you think?"

"I think I would have done anything she might have suggested."

We were silent for a moment and then he said, "Annette's not any better. In fact, they think she's worse."

"I'm sorry." Annette was the Senator's wife. The official diagnosis was paranoid-schizophrenia, but nobody was quite sure because Annette hadn't said a word in four years that I knew of although it must have been six years now. Annette sat quietly in her room in a private sanitarium just outside of Joplin. She would probably sit there the rest of her life.

"I can't get a divorce," Corsing said.

"No."

"I can have a crazy wife in a nut house and nobody minds. I think it even gets me a few votes. It wouldn't have perhaps ten years ago, but it does now. But I can't divorce her and marry someone else and lead a normal life because that would be desertion and senators don't desert their crazy wives. Not yet."

"Wait five years," I said.

"I don't want to wait five years."

"No, I guess not."

"So," he said. "What happened to you?"

"I live on a farm now."

"Harvey."

"Yes."

"I've been out to your farm. We've gotten drunk on your farm. It's a very pretty place but it runs straight up and down a mountain and you couldn't raise a cash crop on it that would pay the light bill.''

"We made almost twelve thousand dollars last year. Almost."

"Off the farm?"

"Well, mostly off of those greeting card things that Ruth does. And my verses. I write greeting card verses now for two dollars a line."

"Jesus."

"We've got two goats," I said.

"Have you thought about food stamps?"

"Food's no problem. Actually, not much of anything is a problem."

"How much did you make the last time you handled something?"

I thought about it. "That would be seventy-two. I made about seventy-five thousand that year. Net. Maybe eighty."

He nodded. "But it wasn't the money. I mean that wasn't really why you were in it."

"No, that wasn't the reason."

"So I'll ask you again. What happened?"

I looked at him and I saw that he wasn't prying. He was seeking information. There was also an expression of mild hope in his eyes as though he thought that I might give him an answer that would enable him to divorce his wife, marry Jenny, move to a hard-scrabble farm in the Ozarks, and tell the voters to get stuffed. If I had done it, perhaps there was a chance, a very small chance, that he could, too.

There wasn't any chance, of course, and he was realistic and honest enough, especially with himself, to know it and that was one of the reasons I liked him. It was also why I decided to tell him the truth. Or what, after nearly four years of thinking about it, I believed to be the truth, which was what would have to serve.

"You really want to know what happened?" I said.

He nodded.

"Well, it just wasn't fun any more. Any of it."

He sighed deeply, nodded again, slumped a little in his

chair, and turned slightly so that he could look out the window. "No," he said softly, "it isn't, is it?"

"Not for me anyhow."

He looked at me again and once more it was the look of an intelligent, puzzled man seeking an answer. "I wonder why it isn't?"

"I'm not quite sure," I said and that's as far as I would go even though he was still looking at me as if he expected something more, something wise perhaps, or even profound. But I had run out of wisdom and profundity nearly four years before, so instead I said, "You're going to go for it again, aren't you? In seventy-eight?"

He looked around his nice corner office. "I will unless somebody offers me a job that pays a lot with a fat pension plan and a big office and a large staff so that I don't have to work too hard and still get to shoot off my mouth all the time and have my name in the paper and my picture on television a lot. You know any jobs around like that?"

"No."

"You know what I wanted to be when I was a kid in St. Louis? A really little kid about seven or eight?"

"President?"

"I wanted to be a short-order cook in a diner. I thought that was kind of classy. I don't think I ever told anyone that before."

"Maybe you ought to tell Jenny," I said.

He thought about it and nodded. "Maybe I should."

There was a silence and then he said, "How'd you get tied up with Roger Vullo's outfit?" Before I could say anything he held up his hand, palm outward like a traffic policeman, and said, "Don't worry, I haven't been running a check on you. Jenny's got a friend that works down at Vullo's place. They gossip a lot. Sometimes it's useful."

"Arch Mix," I said. "Vullo's going to pay me ten thousand dollars to tell him what I think happened to Arch Mix."

"What're you going to do with ten thousand dollars, buy some more goats?"

"I'm going to Dubrovnik."

"Why?"

"I've never been there."

"I thought you'd been everywhere."

"Not to Dubrovnik."

"Arch Mix is dead, isn't he?"

I nodded.

"Any idea why or how?"

"No."

"He was an interesting guy," the Senator said. "He had a good mind, perhaps even a first-class one, although you can never really tell with guys who have jobs that require them to talk all the time."

"It was a good mind," I said.

"He had some interesting theories about civil service reform and the use of the strike by public employees as a collective-bargaining tool."

"His garbage collectors' theory," I said.

"His what?"

"When Mix got elected president of the Public Employees Union twelve years ago it actually wasn't much of a union. It was really more of a polite association, the kind that sponsors the annual city hall picnic. Strike was almost a nasty word. Well, if you're going to have a labour union, you can praise good-faith collective bargaining all you want, but your ultimate weapon is the strike. If the political types that you're bargaining with don't believe that you'll strike because there's a law against public employees striking, then you've lost all your muscle. It's like being in a poker game with no money to call a bluff. So Mix went south."

"Why south?"

"It was a very calculated move. He needed to pull off a successful strike by public employees that would shake up and alter the membership's attitude towards strikes. And he also needed to convince the various mayors and city managers and governors and state legislatures around the country that the PEU was no longer going to be a mild-mannered company union that doted on sweetheart contracts."

"I remember now," Corsing said. "He picked Atlanta."

"In the summer."

"Yes."

"He also picked out the workers who had the least to lose. He picked the garbage collectors."

"What was it, four months?"

"Four months. He took them out in May and he kept them out until September and the union almost went broke. It was the hottest summer in fifty years in Atlanta and the garbage piled up until they swore they could smell it in Savannah."

"They were black, weren't they?"

"The garbage men?" I said. "Ninety-eight per cent of them. At the time I think they were making a buck and a quarter an hour and no overtime. Mix stayed with them all that summer. He slept in their houses, ate with them, and walked the picket line with them. He hated it because he always liked the best hotels and the best restaurants, and carrying a sign in a picket line when the temperature's a hundred and three degrees was his idea of no fun. But he made *Newsweek* and *Time* and the network newscasts were carrying him as though he were sponsored by Exxon."

"And then they put him in the hospital."

I shook my head. "It was only for three days. And the bandages on his head looked good on TV. If you use strikebreakers to bust a strike, you have to pay them something. The city had to pay the ones in Atlanta five bucks an hour which was two and a half bucks more an hour than the garbage men themselves were out on strike for. Well, all that came out after the goons killed four of the garbage men and put Mix in the hospital. By then the garbage was a serious health hazard and the rats had moved in and then they had those three cases of cholera and that did it. The city caved in to all of Mix's demands and this time he made the cover of *Time* and also *Meet the Press*. After that, he and the union were on their way. He took it from a membership of two hundred and fifty thousand to nearly eight hundred thousand and George Meany put him on the AFL-CIO executive council and they started inviting him to parties at the White House when they needed to show off an American labour statesman whose grammar wasn't too bad and who could handle the forks all right. And Mix loved it. Every goddamned minute of it.''

We were silent for a moment and then the Senator said, ''I was back home last week.''

I nodded. Back home was St. Louis.

''The union's pretty strong there.''

''Yes,'' I said. ''Council Twenty-one, I think it is.''

''A guy came to see me. He used to be executive director of the Council.''

''Freddie Koontz?'' I said.

''You know him?''

''I know Freddie. He was one of Mix's original backers. I didn't know he'd retired though. Hell, Freddie can't be more than fifty.''

''He didn't retire,'' the Senator said. ''He got bounced.''

''How'd that happen?''

''Before I tell you that, I'd better mention that the Council's contract with the city expires a couple of weeks from now on September first.''

''So?''

''So when Mix disappeared the Council was in the early stages of negotiating a new contract with the city. A week after Mix disappeared the International sent out about a half-dozen guys from its headquarters here in Washington to help with the negotiations.''

''That's not unusual,'' I said. ''Sometimes the International will send out a team that includes an economist, a lawyer, some resource people, and even some trained negotiators.''

''Freddie would know most of them, wouldn't he?''

''Sure.''

''He didn't know any of this bunch.''

''Who were they?'' I said.

''Freddie still isn't sure. All he knows is that they were very smooth and they had plenty of money and they weren't afraid to use muscle.''

''So how'd it happen?''

''Freddie says that after they were there a week a special

meeting of the Council's board of directors was called. This was right in the middle of negotiations with the city. Well, the first order of business was Freddie. A motion was made to fire him, it was seconded, there was no discussion, the vote was six to five, and Freddie was out of a job. After that they appointed a new executive director. He was a nobody, Freddie said, a rank and filer who knew as much about negotiating a contract as a hog does about a white shirt. I guess you remember how Freddie talks."

"I remember," I said. "Colourfully."

"Well, the Council broke off negotiations, which Freddie said were going pretty well, and two days later they were back with an entirely new set of demands. Freddie says the new demands ask for everything but city hall."

"And the six guys that the International sent out?"

"They're still there. They're calling all the plays now. If any opposition from the membership pops up, they buy it off. Two thousand, three thousand, even as high as five thousand. All cash, or so Freddie says. He also says that when they can't use cash to buy off opposition, they resort to muscle."

"So what does it look like?"

The Senator took out his pipe, filled it, and lit it with a wooden match that he struck against the sole of his left shoe. "It looks like a strike," he said after he puffed on his pipe for a few moments.

"The whole city?"

"Everything but the police and the firemen. The teachers will go out because the Public Employees have the school janitors. Or custodians, I think they're called now."

"Well," I said, "that's interesting."

"It gets better."

"How?"

"My colleague, the distinguished junior senator from Missouri, is scared shitless. If he doesn't carry St. Louis he's dead. Now suppose you were an average voter and a strike by the people whose wages are paid with your hard-earned tax money closed down your schools, interrupted your bus service, shut down your hospitals, eliminated your

garbage collection, screwed up your traffic lights, ended
your street cleaning, and fucked up all the records at city
hall. Now suppose you were that voter and you usually
voted the straight Democratic ticket, how would you vote
come November the second?''

"By gum, I'd vote her straight Republican."

"That's what my distinguished colleague, the junior senator, is scared shitless about."

"He's not the only one who should be scared," I said.
"If the Democrats can't carry St. Louis, they can lose the
whole state. They can't afford to lose any states."

"No," the Senator said, "they can't." He puffed on his
pipe again. "It seems strange to me that a labour union,
which in the past has so publicly aligned itself with the
Democratic party, should call a strike that could well lose
the party a US Senator, not to mention a Congressman or
two, and conceivably, even the presidential election. That
seems strange to me. Passing strange."

"So that's why you asked me to come see you?"

"Yes."

"Mix would never have done it like this, would he?"

"No," the Senator said, "he wouldn't."

"But Arch Mix is no longer with us."

"No."

"It's sort of a motive, isn't it?"

"Barely."

"You haven't gone to anyone else with it, have you?
Such as the FBI?''

Corsing looked up at the ceiling. "Let's suppose the FBI
went clumping around out in St. Louis and the union found
out that they were there at the suggestion of Senator Corsing.
Well, Senator Corsing is up for election in two years and
Senator Corsing would very much like to get re-elected. If
his theory is full of shit, Senator Corsing would much prefer
that nobody found out that it was his theory—especially the
splendid public servants of the great city of St. Louis and
their sizeable bloc of votes."

"So you thought I might do your poking around for
you?"

"You, Harvey, are the logical choice. You knew Arch Mix. You are familiar with the union. In addition, you are intelligent, discreet, totally without ambition, and on somebody else's payroll so you won't cost me a dime. All in all, Harvey, I find you a remarkably felicitous choice."

I rose. "You remember Max Quane, don't you?"

The Senator nodded. "I'm sorry about Max. I heard about it this morning."

"Max called me yesterday just before somebody cut his throat."

"What'd he want?"

"About the same as you. He thought he might have a hunch about what really happened to Arch Mix."

10

The Public Employees Union headquarters was a five-year-old glass and steel cube on G Street between Eighteenth and Nineteenth. It was almost within hailing distance of the White House and only a short, pleasant stroll to the Sans Souci restaurant, which is where Arch Mix had liked to eat lunch, usually in the company of fellow deep thinkers from either the government or the news business or both.

The appointment that Slick had made for me with Warner B. Gallops was for eleven and I arrived five minutes early, but was kept waiting until eleven-twenty. The outer office that I got to wait in was a comfortable place with nicely upholstered furniture, although I thought that Gallops's taste in secretaries was a bit odd.

The secretary was about thirty and he sat behind a desk with nothing on it other than a console telephone and a pad and pencil. Every so often the phone would hum softly, he would pick it up, listen, say "yes" or "no," make a note on his pad, and hang up. It looked like a very soft job for someone who was at least six foot two and weighed about 175 pounds, all of it apparently big bone and hard muscle.

When he wasn't saying yes and no into the phone he sat quietly at his desk with the patient look of a man who has learned how to wait. Once in a while he would flick a glance at me although I don't think I really interested him that much. My one attempt at idle conversation had failed utterly. I had said, "Been with the union long?" He had said, "No, not long," and then he had gone back to waiting for the phone to ring so that he could pick it up and say yes or no.

I took out my tin box, rolled a cigarette, lit it, and thought about Warner Baxter Gallops. I had first met him in the Birmingham bus station in 1964. He and Ward Murfin and I had met there for lunch because back in '64, despite what the Supreme Court said, there still weren't too many public places in Birmingham where two whites and a black could eat without somebody kicking up a fuss. And Murfin and I weren't in Birmingham to desegregate lunch counters. We were there to pick up eight votes.

Warner B. Gallops was not much more than twenty-four then, which would make him thirty-six now. He was a tall, very black, almost shy young man who spoke slowly and carefully as if he weren't too sure of his grammar and was worried about making mistakes. The only one that I ever heard him make was his inevitable use of mens for men, but I had seen no point in correcting him, not if I wanted those eight votes that he had in his hip pocket.

He and Murfin and I had moved down the cafeteria line in the bus station. Gallops had gone first. I remembered looking down the line towards the cashier. She was a white, middle-aged woman with a cheater's eyes and a bitter mouth. Her gaze was fixed on Gallops and the only expression in her eyes was hate, the hot kind that supposedly sears souls.

Without taking her eyes off Gallops, she started ringing our lunches up on the cash register. She didn't look once at our trays to see what we had bought. Nor did she once look at the cash register keys. She just banged away at them, her mouth working a little, as she tried to kill Gallops with her eyes.

When he and Murfin were past her she turned her death gaze on me. By then the hate was hot enough to fry brains. I said, "Nice day." She ripped off the cash register tape and thrust it at me. The total cost of three pretty awful buck-fifty

lunches in the Birmingham bus station came to $32.41, a
net sum that I doubt that I'll ever forget.

There were two things I could do. I could set up a howl
or I could pay. But I wasn't in Birmingham to set up a howl.
I was there to pick up eight votes. So I paid, silent and
perhaps shamefaced, and when I did she grinned spitefully,
the way some people do when they've taken money away
from a coward and said, "Maybe that'll teach you to take
blue-gummed niggers to lunch."

I think I said, "Go fuck yourself, lady," or something
equally trenchant. She gasped a little (it was 1964), but then
she started grinning nastily again because, after all, she had
won and the coward had lost.

When I sat down at the table Gallops said to me, "I'd
sure admire to buy this lunch for you and Brother Murfin."
That's what we were to him then. Brother Murfin and
Brother Longmire. We called him Brother Gallops because
he seemed to think that's what everybody called each other
in labour unions. Dear sir and brother.

"Thanks," I said, "but it didn't cost enough to even
bother about."

"How much did it cost, Brother Longmire?" he said
softly.

"Four-fifty," I said, but when I looked at Gallops I could
see that he knew I had lied and he also knew why. At the
time, I didn't think too much about it.

Over the lunch, Murfin and I told Gallops what a wonderful guy he was and what an equally wonderful future he had
in the union providing that Hundermark got re-elected.
During the previous three years Gallops painfully, all by
himself, without help or encouragement, had put together a
small, all black local of city employees that was either
laughed at or ignored down at Birmingham's city hall. But it
was a local that would have eight votes at the convention
and Gallops would be casting those eight votes.

So we listened to his problems and his hopes and his
dreams and then we assured him that once Hundermark was
re-elected, the International union would bust its collective
ass to see that he had all the organizational help and money

that he could use along with a leased Chevrolet Impala four-door sedan so that he wouldn't have to ride around on the buses any more. But of course all this would happen only if Hundermark got re-elected.

It was our standard pitch and maybe if we hadn't been so tired, we would have caught the flicker in his eyes when he solemnly assured us that he had only the best interest of his local and the International union at heart and that he had nothing but respect and admiration for President Hundermark. Then he had said, "My, my! A Chevrolet Impala *se*dan! Mmmm-mm!" And again, if we hadn't been so tired, we might have caught a trace of the contempt in his voice, but after all it was only eight votes and they seemed pretty safe, and besides, we still had Montgomery, Mobile, Memphis, Little Rock, Baton Rouge, and New Orleans to go.

At the convention Arch Mix had added up the votes and when he found that he might be four short, he had gone to see Warner B. Gallops. But Arch Mix hadn't promised Gallops any Chevrolet Impala sedan. Mix had been too smart for that. He had promised him a vice-presidency instead and that's when Hundermark lost the election. Although sometimes I have thought that Hundermark really lost it that day in the bus station in Birmingham.

I stopped thinking about the past when the door that I had been waiting outside of finally opened. A man came out of it, looked at me thoughtfully, and said, "President Gallops will see you now, Mr. Longmire."

He stood with his back to the door and I almost had to brush up against him to get into Gallops's office. He was a young man, not much more than thirty, if that, and as I went past him I could smell his cologne. It smelled expensive. He smiled at me as I went past but all he really did was stretch his lips without displaying any teeth and I didn't detect any warmth in it.

He closed the door behind us, accompanied me into the large room, and said, "President Gallops, I believe you know Mr. Longmire."

Gallops sat behind a huge desk that once must have belonged to Arch Mix. Gallops didn't get up. He looked up at me without any pleasure that I could see and said, "Yeah, we know each other."

"Why don't you sit down over here, Mr. Longmire, where you'll be comfortable," the young man said and indicated one of the four or five chairs that were drawn up around Gallops's desk. Then he said, "I think I'll just sit over here." The chair that he picked for himself was the one nearest Gallops.

I sat down, looked at Gallops, nodded my head towards the young man, and said, "Who's he?"

"I'm sorry, Mr. Longmire, I forgot to introduce myself. I'm Ralph Tutor, President Gallops's executive assistant."

"Is he new?" I said to Gallops.

"That's right," Gallops said. "He's new."

"Where'd you find him?" I said.

The young man who said his name was Ralph Tutor smiled again and this time I was given a good look at his teeth. They were very white and shiny and almost square. "I formerly was with the government," he said, "but that was some years ago. Most recently I've been associated with a firm of management consultants here in Washington."

"That sounds exciting," I said and then asked Gallops, "What do you think, Warner, is Arch dead?"

Gallops rose, went over to the window, and looked out. He was still just as tall as I remembered, and just as black, but he no longer seemed shy. "Yeah, I think he's dead," he said. "I think somebody killed him."

"Why?"

He turned. "That's what I'm paying that uncle of yours to find out. The cops haven't come up with any answers and neither has the FBI. So that's why I hired your uncle, although I sure as shit didn't know he was your uncle when I hired him."

"We've also posted a one-hundred-thousand-dollar reward for any information that leads to the discovery of what really has happened to President Mix," Tutor said and frowned. "So far we've heard from no one but cranks."

Gallops returned to his high-backed swivel chair, slumped down into it, and swivelled back and forth, his eyes not leaving my face. "A lot of the nuts that write or call in suggest that I got rid of Arch—or had it done," he said. "We turn all of the stuff that we get like that over to the cops. Well, you can imagine what kind of questions they've asked me."

"Yes," I said, "I can."

"I've had to go back and try and remember every goddamn move I've made for the past six months almost. So that's why I hired your uncle. Not just to find out what the hell happened to Arch, but to prove I had fuck all to do with it—whatever it was."

"You've got no idea, right?" I said.

"None."

"May I ask just what your interest might be in President's Mix's disappearance, Mr. Longmire?"

I looked at Tutor. He had deep-set dark eyes that glittered a bit above a nose that hooked down slightly towards a wide, thin-lipped mouth that I found just a little too pink, although I was probably being picky. The mouth rested on a stubborn chin. It was a lean, mobile face that most people probably found intelligent. I thought it looked crafty.

"The Vullo Foundation," I said. "The Vullo Foundation is interested in conspiracies and they think that Arch Mix's disappearance might just be one so they're paying me to look into it and tell them what I think."

"And what *do* you think, Mr. Longmire?" Tutor said. "Do you think there is a conspiracy?"

"I haven't decided," I said, "but when I do, I'll let everybody know."

"President Mix's disappearance is really rather a family concern of yours, isn't it?" Tutor said. "I mean there's your uncle, and yourself, of course, and then there's your sister." He smiled again. "You did know about your sister and President Mix?"

"Yes, it's been quite a family scandal," I said. "Heartbreak all around." I looked at Gallops. "What kind of shape did Arch leave you in?"

"Rotten," he said.

"How so?"

"He got this idea about three years ago that he was going to re-schedule all our big contracts. You know, Chicago, L.A., New York and the rest of the real big ones."

"St. Louis?" I said.

"Yeah, St. Louis, too. Well, Arch's idea was that if we could get them all re-scheduled to expire at about the same time, we would have a national instead of a local impact, you know what I mean?"

"How's it working out?"

Gallops shook his head. "It's a goddamn mess. This is the first time out that we've had ten, maybe a dozen big city contracts all being negotiated at once and, shit, the first thing I found out was that we just weren't staffed to handle it."

"So what'd you do?" I said. "Hire some new people?"

"Had to."

"Where'd you find them?"

"Wherever I could." Gallops nodded at Tutor. "That consultancy outfit that he used to work for has been a big help. In fact, that's where I got him. I mean, hell, you just don't go out on the street and tap some guy on the shoulder and say, 'Hey, pal, how'd you like to run over to Pittsburgh and help negotiate a new contract with the city for us?'"

I smiled at Tutor and tried to make myself seem both earnest and sincere. "That must be quite an organization that you worked for."

"Yes, it is, although I must say I find my new association with President Gallops to be both immensely stimulating and rewarding."

"I can imagine," I said. "I don't think you mentioned the name of the firm that you were with."

"No, I didn't, did I?"

"No."

"Would you like me to?"

"I'm just curious."

"It's called Douglas Chanson Associates."

I turned back to Gallops. "You certainly were lucky to find somebody like that."

Gallops grunted. "They didn't come free."

"How many people have they hired for you?"

He looked at Tutor. "I'd say about two hundred, wouldn't you?"

Tutor nodded.

"Jesus," I said, "who's paying them?"

"We are, Mr. Longmire," Tutor said, "although we are rather extending ourselves to do it."

"If you put two hundred guys on the payroll," I said, "you're going to have to pay them each at least fifteen thousand a year. That's a three-million-dollar payroll right there and they haven't even turned in their expense accounts yet, which they sure as hell will."

"They'll pay for themselves," Gallops said.

"How?"

"Really, Mr. Longmire," Tutor said. "When President Gallops agreed to give you an appointment, I don't think he was expecting you to deliver a critique of his administration of the union. As we understood it, you were solely concerned with the disappearance of President Mix. I fail to see how that, tragic as it may be, has anything to do with the union's current affairs."

"Does he always talk as pretty as that?" I said to Gallops.

"Maybe I'd better translate for you," Gallops said and leaned forward, his elbows on his desk, his hands clasped in front of him. "What he's saying, Harvey, is that Arch isn't around any more and that's a real shame, but the union's still got business to do, Arch or no Arch, and somebody's got to handle that business and that somebody is me. Not Arch. Just me. You understand what I'm saying?"

"Perfectly," I said and rose. "Well, gentlemen, thank you for your time and I certainly wish you luck, which somehow I feel you're going to need a lot of."

"Mr. Longmire," Tutor said.

"Yes."

"If you do find evidence of some dreadful conspiracy, you will let us know, won't you?"

"You'll be among the first," I said and turned away.

"Harvey," Gallops said. I turned again. He was leaning

back in his chair, staring up at me, a look of honest puzzlement on his face.

"What?" I said.

"You didn't used to wear a moustache, did you?"

"No."

"I didn't think so. You know who it makes you look like?"

"Who?"

He snapped his fingers a couple of times as if trying to remember. "He was a real old-time movie actor. Started with an H."

"Holt," Tutor said. "It makes him look something like Jack Holt."

I looked at him. "You're not old enough to remember Jack Holt."

He smiled pleasantly. Or maybe it was craftily. "That's right, Mr. Longmire, I'm not."

11

Slick was in a mild snit because he had forgotten to bring any salt. Our luncheon appointment was taking place on a bench under the shade of some trees along the north rim of Dupont Circle. Slick had brought his lunch in a proper wicker basket that was covered with a red and white checked cloth. Mine was contained in a brown paper sack. I reached into the sack and handed him a twist of paper that held some salt. He thanked me and sprinkled a pinch of it on his cold broiled breast of chicken.

"Sometimes, Harvey," he said, "you do have perfectly splendid ideas. I don't really believe that I've been on a picnic in years."

"Would you like some of my cheese?"

He looked at it suspiciously. "Is that some of your goat cheese?"

"It's a kind of Brie."

"Kind of?"

"Yes."

"Well, dear boy, I really do think I shall pass."

My lunch consisted of the cheese, two hard-boiled eggs, a tomato, and some cold biscuits left over from dinner the night before. Slick's was somewhat more grand. There was the chicken breast; a portion of pâté that he said he had made himself and insisted that I try; a small salad; half a loaf of French bread; some assorted olives; and a Thermos full of a chilled, light Moselle that he said was a particularly good buy that year. We didn't drink the wine out of any tacky paper cups, however. We drank it the way it should be drunk, out of two long-stemmed wine glasses that Slick had packed in the wicker basket.

While we ate I told him about how I'd found Max Quane with his throat cut and why I hadn't waited around for the police, none of which seemed to disturb Slick's appetite in the least.

"And it was really one of Nicole's old spoons?" Nicole had been my mother's name.

"Yes."

"And the girl—uh—Sally. I do have a problem with that young woman's name."

"Sally Raines."

"Yes. Raines. She hasn't returned to Audrey's since receiving that phone call yesterday?"

"No."

"So it would seem that the late Mr. Quane purposely wooed Miss Raines so that he could use her to pry information about Arch Mix out of Audrey. Pillow-talk information, I suppose one should call it. The fellow must have been something of a cad."

"Mix was something like that," I said, wondering when I had last heard somebody called a cad.

"I wonder what Mr. Quane found out that would necessitate someone cutting his throat?"

"I don't know. But those two guys who were watching Audrey's house yesterday must have been watching it for Sally, not Audrey."

"Yes. So it would seem."

"And now you know why I decided that I'd better see a lawyer," I said.

Slick sipped his wine and thought about it. "Yes," he said. "I really do think you should. Of course, I can drop a word here and there that might make things a bit easier for you when you describe your rather aberrant behaviour to the police."

"I'd be grateful," I said.

"They won't welcome you with loving arms, you understand."

"No."

"On the other hand, they probably won't clap you in jail, either."

"That's nice. Ruth will appreciate that. So will the goats."

"Anything else?"

"Well, I saw your client today."

"And how was Mr. Gallops?"

"He's taken over, hasn't he?"

"Oh, quite. I don't think he hesitated more than a day or two after Mix disappeared before he assumed full direction of the union's affairs. But then, someone had to."

"What kind of board of directors did Mix have?"

"A tame one, so I understand," Slick said. "Very carefully assembled over the years."

"So Gallops needn't worry about them?"

"No, but why should he?"

"He's spending a lot of money."

"Really?"

I told Slick about the 200 full-time representatives that Gallops had put on the union's payroll, and why, and his reaction was similar to mine. "However, Harvey," he said, "I think that your estimate of the total cost is a bit low. It would be closer to four million a year than three million."

"A lot of money."

"A great deal," he said. "I wonder just how one would go about finding two hundred such people? I mean, they would have to have some experience with or at least some affinity for a labour union, wouldn't they?"

"Not necessarily," I said. "From what I've heard so far all they'd really have to be good at is convincing a limited group of people to do what they want them to do. And labour union members are no different from anyone else. You can get them to do what you'd like them to do by the skilled use of persuasion and sweet reason. But if that fails, you can always fall back on coercion, bribery, and maybe just muscle, which seems to be what some of Gallops's new guys are using.''

''I see. Did Gallops say where he'd found them?''

''He said an outfit called Douglas Chanson Associates found them for him. Ever heard of it?''

''The headhunter,'' Slick said.

''Oh?''

''Yes, he started about ten years ago, I believe, and has done remarkably well ever since.''

''You know him?''

''We've met on several occasions.''

''Slick?''

''Yes, dear boy?''

''He didn't used to be with the agency, did he?''

''Chanson? Certainly not. He got his start, as I said, about ten years ago in what was then a rather ripe field. His speciality was supplying certain government agencies and private industry with competent, middle-management executives. As I said, Chanson is a headhunter. However, he specialized in supplying his clients with *black* middle-management executives. He did extremely well, or so I understand. Later, when the women's movement—uh, burgeoned, shall we say, he supplied his ever-expanding list of clients with *female* middle-management executives and, recently, or so the rumours have it, he's been doing rather nicely by coming up with executives who are both black *and* female.''

''But that's not all he does?''

''Oh, certainly not. He also helps solve those little problems that are always popping up in both government and industry. Labour relations, I understand, just happen to be one of his many specialities.''

''And you're sure he didn't used to be with the agency?''

''I'm quite sure. For fifteen years Douglas Chanson was a top special agent with the FBI.''

Slick took the last sip of the wine, collected our glasses, and tucked them back into the wicker basket. He then shook the crumbs from the red and white checked cloth, folded it carefully, and laid it on top of the glasses. As always, he was very neat.

"So," I said, "what else have you got for me?"

"Well, dear boy, right now I am involved in one particular aspect of this affair, but unfortunately I can't give you any details because, well, because it just might jeopardize everything."

"What's everything?"

"I can't tell you that either."

"We're supposed to have a trade-off, Slick. But so far it's been mostly a one-way deal. I give and you take."

"Well, I can give you just one tiny hint," he said, "but only if you swear to keep it absolutely confidential. Agreed?"

"All right," I said.

"And I positively will not tell you any more than I'm going to tell you so there's no use in your asking. Understood?"

"Sure."

He looked up at the hot August sky as if trying to decide how best to phrase his tiny hint. Then he said, "Well, there seems to be a slight possibility that Arch Mix isn't dead after all."

* * *

Ward Murfin looked as if he hadn't had much sleep. When his secretary, Ginger, showed me into his office at the Vullo Foundation, Murfin was stretched out on the couch. He wasn't asleep though. He was smoking a cigarette and staring up at the ceiling. His eyes were red and swollen and for a moment I wondered whether he had been crying until I thought about it and decided that Murfin probably hadn't cried about anything since he was five years old. Maybe four.

He waved his cigarette at me by way of greeting and then said to Ginger, "Would you get us some coffee, honey?" Ginger said, "Of course," and gave him a concerned, tender look which made me decide that Murfin was probably sleeping with her. I would have been more surprised if he hadn't because Murfin always slept with his secretaries. Or at least tried to. He felt that it was an automatic fringe benefit that went with the job along with two-hour lunches, a pension plan, four-week vacations, a company car, and hospital insurance.

Murfin stretched, yawned, lowered his feet to the floor, and sat up. He held his cigarette between his lips while he rubbed his eyes. When he was done they were more bleary than ever.

"You know what time we got home this morning?" he said.

"What time?"

"Four-thirty. That's after me and Marjorie finally got Dorothy to bed. She was almost out on her feet by then, but she was still talking about killing herself. Jesus, I think she gets her kicks out of talking about it."

"For some people the thought of suicide is a comfort," I said. "It gets them through their tough spots. The thought of it comforts them because it offers an ultimate solution to all their problems."

Murfin looked at me with disbelief. "Where'd you come up with a horseshit theory like that?"

"From Dorothy," I said. "We used to talk about suicide sometimes. Usually on Sunday afternoon. Usually it was raining. It cheered her up. Talking about it, I mean."

"Shit, I never thought about killing myself," Murfin said and I believed him. He doubtless lumped suicide with devil worship, witchcraft, animal sodomy, group therapy and other wicked pursuits that he felt to be crimes against both man and nature.

Ginger came in with the coffee, served us, and left. Murfin took a noisy sip of his and said, "Well, anyway we get home at four-thirty, but do I get to go to sleep? Hell, no. Marjorie's gotta sit up until six o'clock analysing it. She isn't interested in why Max went and got himself killed. Oh, no. What she's interested in is analysing what she keeps calling Max's manipulative relationship with Dorothy which is what she claims is the real reason that Dorothy wants to kill herself. Well, poor old Max is lying down there dead with his throat cut and I can't find anybody to be his pallbearers, but Marjorie's gotta sit up until six o'clock in the fuckin' morning blaming Max for Dorothy's saying she wants to kill herself, which now you tell me is what makes Dorothy feel better. Jesus.''

"I'll go see her this afternoon," I said. "After I go see the police and tell them how I found Max."

"*You* found him?" Murfin said as something seemed to wipe the tiredness from his eyes.

"I think I'd better tell you about it," I said. "In fact, I think I'd better tell you about everything."

So I told him and when I was through he wanted more details, so I fed them to him until he was almost sated, except that my mother's silver spoon seemed to fascinate him. I had to explain several times how I could tell that it was one of her spoons. He finally accepted my explanation with the comment that, "Well, hell, maybe you could, I don't know. We never had no silver spoons in my house when I was a kid anyway."

"I could tell it was her spoon," I said. "Believe me."

"Yeah, okay, you could tell. So what do you think?"

"I think I want to be paid one half in advance. Five thousand dollars."

"What the hell for?"

"Because, like Max, I don't have any insurance and if I keep on poking around and, like Max, come up with a hot idea about what really happened to Arch Mix, then somebody might decide to cut my throat, which would leave my wife a very poor widow."

"Aw, shit, Harvey."

"I'm serious," I said.

"Okay, we'll check it with Vullo."

"Good."

Murfin took another loud sip of his coffee, put the cup down, lit another cigarette, stretched, leaned back on the couch, and looked up at the ceiling. "You say Gallops put two hundred guys on the payroll," he said. "How do you figure that?"

"I figure," I said, "that you and I had better take a run out to St. Louis."

Murfin stopped looking at the ceiling and instead looked at me. He nodded happily, gave me one of his more knavish smiles, and said, "Yeah, that's just what I was figuring."

* * *

Roger Vullo listened with rapt attention as I gave him the same report that I had given Murfin. I knew Vullo's attention was rapt because he forgot to bite his fingernails. However, when I was through, or thought I was through, he wanted even more details than Murfin had demanded although Vullo didn't seem to find it at all strange that I could recognize one of my mother's old silver spoons. But then Roger Vullo had had silver spoons in his house when he was a kid.

One of the details that Vullo was especially interested in was how Max Quane had looked as he had crawled from the bathroom into the living room to die on the cheap green rug.

"He didn't say anything before he died?" Vullo asked.

"No. He was pretty far gone."

"Not a word?"

"No."

"Poor Quane," Vullo said and I think that was the only expression of sympathy or regret that I ever heard him make about Max Quane.

It was Murfin who broached the subject of paying me half of my ten-thousand-dollar fee in advance. Vullo listened quietly to my reasoning although he started nibbling at his fingernails again. The little finger on his left hand seemed to be giving him particular trouble. When I was through with my pitch, he picked up his phone, spoke quietly into it, and then looked at me after he hung it up. "The cheque will be in shortly, Mr. Longmire."

"Thank you."

"You really do feel that you might be in some danger?"

"I hope not, but there may be the possibility."

"How does it make you feel?" he said. I thought it was a

strange question, but when I looked at him carefully I could detect only real interest, although it may have contained a trace of prurience.

"Nervous," I said. "Watchful. Apprehensive. Perhaps even a little frightened."

"Paranoiac?"

"Maybe, a little, but I don't really think so."

Vullo nodded thoughtfully. "You know, I've never been in any real danger that I can think of. It must be interesting."

"Yes," I said. "Extremely."

"Now, then," he said, all brisk business again, "this trip to St. Louis. When do you think you might go?"

I looked at Murfin. "Tomorrow?"

"Yeah, tomorrow. They aren't going to bury old Max until day after tomorrow. We ought to be back in time." He looked at Vullo and then asked in the tone of a man who has just been struck by an absolutely brilliant idea. "How'd you like to be a pallbearer at Max's funeral?"

The idea caused Vullo to make a savage attack on his right thumbnail with his teeth. When he had won he looked up at Murfin and said without a trace of regret, "I'm extremely sorry, but I really don't think that my relationship with Quane was quite that personal."

"That's the trouble," Murfin said with a sigh. "I can't find anybody who thinks they and Max had anything personal going."

"Surely Mr. Longmire knew Quane quite well."

"Harvey?" Murfin said. "Harvey don't go to funerals."

That was a new fact and new facts always interested Vullo. He looked at me and said, "Why not?"

"I no longer do things that I don't like to do, if I can avoid doing them. I can avoid going to funerals. So I don't."

Vullo thought that over and to help his thoughts along he bit the nail on his right index finger. "I think I find that a rather irresponsible attitude," he said finally.

"So do I," I said, "but being responsible to anyone other than myself and my family is one of the things I now avoid because I never liked it anyhow."

"You're very blunt."

"I see no reason not to be."

"No, I don't either," Vullo said. "In fact, it's rather refreshing. However, we do have a problem that you may be able to help us with. I trust you won't mind giving us your thoughts?"

"Not at all."

"We need to find a replacement for Quane," he said. "I think you'll agree that he had certain singular qualities that will make replacing him rather difficult."

If Roger Vullo wouldn't mourn for Max Quane, at least he would miss him—or his singular qualities, which consisted largely of a quick, cunning mind, a thoroughly manipulative personality, a streak of utter ruthlessness, and an unerring eye for other people's weaknesses. If he had really wanted to, Max Quane could probably have been a highly successful business executive, or if that were too tame, a Hollywood agent.

I thought about where Vullo might find himself another Max Quane and then I had an idea. But before I could tell him about it his secretary came in with the cheque. She handed it to Vullo who scrawled his name on it and then moved it across his huge desk to Murfin who signed with something of a flourish and handed it to me. I looked at it, saw that it was for five thousand dollars, and put it in my pocket.

Vullo dismissed his secretary with a curt nod and when she was gone I said, "I've heard about someone who might be able to help you find a replacement for Max. He's a headhunter."

"What's that?" Vullo said, not at all ashamed of his ignorance.

"Someone who specializes in finding just the right person to fill hard-to-fill jobs. In fact, the one that I'm thinking of was the one who somehow located those two hundred guys that the union's hired. His name's Douglas Chanson although he calls himself Douglas Chanson Associates."

Vullo gave his right thumbnail a nasty nip. "How very curious that you should mention Chanson," he said.

"Why curious?"

"He's a friend of mine and when I was just starting the Foundation I went to him for advice and counsel. And it was he that recommended Murfin here." Vullo looked at Murfin. "I never told you that, did I?"

"No," Murfin said, "you never did."

"Douglas suggested that I be discreet in my approach to you, so I was. You don't mind, do you?"

"No," Murfin said, "I don't mind."

"So perhaps Mr. Longmire has a good suggestion. I think I will get in touch with Douglas again. What do you think, Murfin?"

"Whatever's right," Murfin said.

I could see that our meeting with Vullo was over, at least as far as he was concerned, so rather than risk one of his peremptory dismissals, I started to get up. I was almost halfway there when the phone rang. Vullo frowned, picked it up, said, "I see," looked at me, and frowned again. "It's for you," he said. "Would you mind taking it in Murfin's office?"

"Not at all," I said and headed for the door with Murfin close behind me. When we reached his office I picked up the phone and said hello. It was my sister and she sounded frantic, or as near to frantic as Audrey would ever permit herself to be.

"All right, calm down," I said. "What's the matter?"

"Sally called."

"So?"

"She wants to come home."

"Well, good."

"She sounded awful."

"What do you mean awful?"

"How the hell do I know what I mean by awful? She sounded scared and mixed up and desperate and, I don't know, panicky, I reckon. She wanted me to come get her."

"Why doesn't she take a cab?"

"Goddamn it, Harvey, I told you she's scared out of her mind. She wants me to come get her, but I can't leave the kids and I don't want to take them over there so I told her I'd get you to go.''

"Where's over there?'' I said.

"It's over on Twelfth Street Southeast.'' She read the number to me. It wasn't much of a neighbourhood. "I didn't want to take the kids over there.''

"No,'' I said, "I don't think you should. When did she call?''

"About ten minutes ago. Maybe fifteen. I called Slick and he said you might still be at Vullo's.''

"Did Sally say anything else?''

"Like what, damn it?''

"I don't know. Anything?''

"She just said she wanted to come home,'' Audrey said. "Isn't that enough?''

"Sure it is,'' I said. "I'll go get her.''

"Right away?''

"Right away.''

I told my sister good-bye and hung up. I turned to Murfin. "You want to take a little ride?'' I said.

"Where to?'' he said.

"Over on Twelfth Street Southeast. Max's girl friend is there. She wants to go home to my sister's except that she's too scared to take a cab.''

Murfin looked at me. "The spade fox,'' he said thoughtfully.

"That's right.''

"Think maybe she can tell us something about Max?''

"We can ask,'' I said.

"Yeah, we can, can't we,'' he said. "Okay, let's go.'' He started towards the door, then stopped, and turned back to me. "You know something?''

"What?''

"When we get back from our little run out to St. Louis, maybe you and me had better check out this Douglas Chanson Associates guy. What do you think?''

"I think you're right,'' I said.

12

We took Murfin's car, the big brown 450 SEL Mercedes that he drove carelessly, almost recklessly, the way a lot of people drive leased cars, secure in the knowledge that somebody else will have to pay for the skinned paint or the nicked bumper.

"You wanta know something?" Murfin said.

"What?"

"I like this car better'n any car I ever had except one. You wanta know what that one was?"

"A 1959 Cadillac convertible that you had when you were nineteen," I said. "It was yellow."

"I already told you about it?" He sounded disappointed.

"You already told me."

He told me again anyway.

When Murfin was graduated from high school in 1956 he hadn't gone on to college because there hadn't been any money to send him and because he really hadn't wanted to go anyway. Instead he had gone to work for something called the Acme Novelty Company in Pittsburgh. The Acme Novelty Company supplied Pittsburgh with most of its pinball machines, which were legal, and with all of its slot machines, which weren't.

The principal owner of the Acme Novelty Company was one Francesco Salleo, quite often referred to in the Pittsburgh papers as Filthy Frankie, who was alleged to have certain important connections Back East (New York) and Out West (Las Vegas). Filthy Frankie was quick to recognize Murfin's genuine mechanical ability, as well as his flair for sound business practices. As a result Murfin quickly went up the promotional ladder at the Acme Novelty Company and soon was in charge of the placement and servicing of all slot machines in Pittsburgh's numerous fraternal halls, country clubs, veterans' posts, after-hours joints, and whorehouses.

As a reward for his diligence, ability and unswerving loyalty to the firm, Filthy Frankie rewarded Murfin, by then nineteen, with a salary of $500 a week, not an insignificant sum to a nineteen-year-old back in 1957, or, for that matter, today.

It was with his newly gained prosperity that Murfin purchased the 1957 yellow Cadillac convertible, a car remembered, if not cherished, for its enormous tail fins. In it he went courting Miss Marjorie Bzowski, eighteen, daughter of Big Mike Bzowski, business agent for Local 12 of the United Steelworkers of America (AFL-CIO).

Filthy Frankie was to have been best man at the marriage of Murfin and Miss Bzowski and doubtless would have been had he not been found floating in the Monongahela River on the wedding day, the back of his head blown off by a shotgun blast.

Frankie's connections Back East (New York) started feuding over the spoils with his connections Out West (Las Vegas) and the feud developed into a minor war that left dead bodies about. Murfin, forced to take sides in the war, unfortunately chose the wrong side. As a result he was hauled before a grand jury, but with the aid of an expensive lawyer he managed to escape being indicted. However, it cost him his job, his savings, and his treasured 1957 yellow Cadillac convertible.

Burdened, or perhaps blessed, with a young wife who was expecting their first child Murfin took the only job he could get. It was obtained for him in a Pittsburgh steel mill by his father-in-law. It was a job that required Murfin to rise early, work hard, get his hands dirty, and he loathed it. He soon saw that union officials had to work nowhere nearly as hard as did the rank and file members and within a year he was secretary-treasurer of his local union.

Soon after that he went on the steelworkers' payroll as a fulltime organizer. He was an excellent organizer and in 1960 when he was twenty-two he switched to the Public Employees Union. By the time he was twenty-six he was the PEU's Director of Organization.

"You know," he said as we drove east on Pennsylvania Avenue, "that was the best goddamn job I ever had in my life, that time when I was with Frankie."

"You're lucky you didn't get killed," I said.

"I don't know," he said, "if Frankie could've stayed alive, there's no telling where I might be today."

"Vice lord of Pittsburgh, huh?"

He looked at me. "What's wrong with that?"

"Not a thing," I said.

When we got to Twelfth and Pennsylvania Avenue we turned right, drove a block, and started looking for a place to park. The house number that Audrey had given me was in the middle of a block that so far had resisted the renaissance of Capitol Hill which seemed bent on turning the area into another Georgetown. The renaissance meant, in effect, that a house that a speculator bought for $15,000 in 1970 would, with a little renovation, command an $80,000 price today.

The block that we parked in was a sullen stretch of row houses, most of them three storeys tall and most of them in evident need of paint. It was largely an all-black block lined with ageing cars. Some of the cars had no wheels and some of them had no doors and nearly all of them that had no wheels or doors had no glass. Some kids played in and near several of the cars but they didn't play very hard. At three o'clock on an August afternoon in Washington it was too hot to play hard.

When we got out of the Mercedes Murfin made sure that all of the doors were locked. He loosened his tie and I wondered whether he had picked it out that morning while he was still asleep. It was a big, wide fat orange and green tie that screamed and fought for attention with a French blue shirt, a reddish plaid jacket, and lilac windowpane slacks. I also wondered if Murfin were colourblind. It was something that I had often wondered.

The house that we were looking for was in a little better condition than most of its neighbours. It was three storeys tall with an English basement and somebody had bothered to give it a coat of fresh white paint and put new screens on all the windows. The house also boasted a covered porch with a wooden railing. A man in an undershirt sat on the porch in a tilted-back kitchen chair, his feet up on the railing, a can of beer in his hand. He was a black man of about sixty with close cropped white frizzy hair. He sat underneath a dime-store sign that advertised rooms for rent.

Murfin and I headed for the cement walk that split the narrow, shallow front yard in half and led to the house. The yard had a few patches of brown grass that seemed to have given up and died in the August heat. The rest of the yard was hard-packed brown dirt in which nothing could grow. For decoration there were a few empty bottles that nobody had bothered to collect yet.

We heard the scream when we were about twenty feet from the walk that led to the house. The man on the porch heard it, too, because the front legs of his tilted-back chair came down on the porch floor with a hard crack. He turned his head as if he could look into his house and see who was screaming.

The screen door flew open and she burst out of the house, all pale brown and dark red from the blood that ran from her nose and mouth down her chin to her throat and her breasts. She raced down the steps of the porch to the sidewalk and paused. She looked down at herself and touched the blood that had reached her bare breasts. She stared at the blood for a moment and then almost absently wiped it on the side of her leg. The leg was bare, too, as was the rest of her. Sally Raines was naked.

I yelled, "Sally!" and she looked my way, but I don't think she really saw me. Her eyes jumped from me back to the house. She threw her head back and screamed again. It was a long scream that rang of terror and panic and near hysteria.

In the middle of her scream the door opened and the two men with the guns came out. They wore ski masks. One mask was blue and the other was red and I remember thinking that ski masks in August must be hot and sweaty.

The man with the red mask waved his gun almost idly at the white-haired black man who still clutched his can of beer. The black man shrank back, pressing himself against the wall.

The man in the blue mask moved quickly and smoothly down the three porch steps. He went into a crouch and used both hands to aim his pistol. It was a revolver with what looked like a six-inch barrel. He aimed it at Sally Raines.

She stopped screaming and started to run. She ran down the sidewalk. I snatched up an empty pint bottle that had once contained Old Overholt, a pretty good rye. I threw it sidearmed and I threw it hard. The bottle glittered, spinning in the August sun, as it flew at the man in the blue ski mask who was aiming his pistol at Sally Raines. It hit him high on the left arm. A lucky throw. It didn't make him drop his pistol. It just made him look at me. He changed his stance with a jump and came down in a crouch again, his pistol aimed at my head or my heart. It was hard to tell. I didn't move.

The other man, the one in the red ski mask, glanced our way almost casually and then slowly raised his pistol with both hands. He took his time. He shot Sally Raines twice in the back and once in the head as she ran down the sidewalk. The first bullet struck her in the small of the back and her arms went out and up towards the sky as though there was something up there that she wanted to touch. The second shot slammed into her left shoulder and spun her around in a curiously graceful motion, almost like a pirouette. The third shot went into her face, just below her left eye, and she may have been dead by the time she crumpled to the ground although they say that it takes longer than that to die.

The man who had shot Sally Raines looked at Murfin and

me. Then he moved over and touched the other man on the shoulder. The other man nodded and started backing towards the house, still pointing his gun at me. The two men turned and disappeared through the screen door, letting it slam behind them.

I didn't move for a while. Neither did Murfin. The man on the porch slowly raised his beer can to his mouth. Another screen door slammed. It seemed to come from the rear of the house. A moment or two later we heard a car engine start. And then we heard a car drive off.

They started coming out of their houses then. They came singly and in groups of two or three to stare down at the dead young woman who lay awkwardly on the sidewalk. At first they murmured about it and then their voices rose as they started telling each other what had happened. One of them, a woman of about fifty, started to sob.

I turned to Murfin. "I've got to get to a phone," I said. He nodded. "That was her?"

"Yes," I said. "That was Sally Raines."

I started towards the porch where the man with the beer can still stood. "You got a phone?" I said.

"That mother almost shot you," he said. "When you went and threw that bottle he almost shot you."

"You got a phone?" I said again.

"Yeah, I got a phone." He took another swallow of his beer and started into the house. Murfin and I followed. "You must be fuckin' crazy, man, throwin' somethin' at a man with a gun," the man with the beer said over his shoulder, then stopped, turned, and looked at me. "Pretty good throw though."

He led us into the house and we turned right into a living room where a large colour-console television set played silently to some unseen audience.

"Phone's over there," he said.

I picked up the phone and made my first call. When Audrey answered I said, "I've got some bad news. Some very bad news. Sally's been shot. She's dead."

There was a silence and then she whispered, "Ohmygodno."

"There's nothing you can do for her."

"When did it happen?"

"Just a few minutes ago."

"Oh, shit, it's my fault. It's all my goddamn fault."

"Audrey!" I said, barking her name.

"Yes," she said, her voice still almost a whisper.

"It's not your fault. It's not your fault at all. Listen, I want you to do something and I want you to do it right now."

"What?"

"I want you to throw some clothes together for you and the kids and I want you to get in your car and drive out to the farm. Ruth'll be there."

"Ruth'll be there?" The shock of Sally Raines's death must have hit then because her voice had gone dull and childlike, although it sounded pleased about Ruth.

"She'll be expecting you and the kids," I said.

"You want us to go to the farm?"

"Yes."

"Are you going to be there?"

"I'll be there later."

"You want us to go now?"

"That's right."

"And Ruth'll be there."

There was another silence and then she said in a low, tortured voice, "Oh, God, Harvey, why'd it all have to happen?"

"We'll talk about it later. At the farm."

"At the farm," she said and then hung up without saying goodbye.

I put the phone down and looked around the room. The black man was staring at his television set. "I don't much watch it, y'know. I just kinda like the colours all moving around. I reckon it's sorta like a fireplace."

"Where'd the other guy go?" I said.

"The other guy? He went upstairs. He went upstairs because he wanted to pee and because he wanted to look at her room. Shit, I don't wanta look at her room, do you?"

"No," I said, picked up the phone and made a collect call to Ruth. When she answered I told her about Sally

Raines and that Audrey and the children would be coming out to stay for a while.

"I'm terribly sorry about Sally," Ruth said. "She and Audrey were so close. Is Audrey all right?"

"She might need a little comforting."

"Of course." There was a pause and then Ruth said, "Did you see it happen?"

"Yes. Murfin and I saw it. We're going to have to talk to the police."

"Harvey?"

"Yes."

"Don't take any more chances. It's not worth it."

"No," I said, "it really isn't."

After we said good-bye I made my third call. It was to my lawyer, Earl Inch. When he came on I said, "I think I'm in even more trouble than I thought I was."

"Excellent," he said and when I told him about it and where I was he said he would be right over. "Have you called the cops?" he asked.

I could hear a siren somewhere. It seemed to be coming closer. "No," I said. "Somebody else did."

After talking to Inch I turned from the phone just as Murfin came into the room. The white-haired black had got himself another can of beer and was drinking it as he stood staring reflectively into the silent colour of the television set that served as his surrogate fireplace. Murfin looked at the man, then at me, and jerked his head towards the door, indicating that he wanted us to go outside. I nodded, thanked the man for the use of his phone, and went out onto the porch with Murfin.

"Jesus, I had to piss," he said.

"What was her room like?"

He shook his head. "Her clothes were lying all over everything. Looked like they tore 'em off her. What does Chad mean?"

"How do you spell it?"

He spelled it for me.

"It's the name of a country in Africa. It also could be a

man's name, usually his first name, although it's not too common. You know anybody named Chad?''

"No."

"Why do you want to know?''

"There was a little old beat-up desk in her room. There were a couple of pieces of paper on it, all wadded up. There wasn't anything on one of them. But on the other somebody'd written down Chad. It looked like a girl's writing.''

"Jesus," I said, "maybe it's a clue.''

"Yeah," Murfin said happily. "Maybe it is.''

13

Detective Aaron Oxley of the Metropolitan Police Department's homicide squad couldn't think of anything to charge me with except a felony that could, he said, get me five to ten years in Lorton. The felony that Detective Oxley had in mind was my failure to report a felony. The felony that I had failed to report was Max Quane's murder, but my lawyer, Earl Inch, pooh-poohed that as only a $100-an-hour lawyer can; with magnificent derision and chilling disdain. Detective Oxley took it well enough because he really didn't seem too interested in charging me with anything anyhow. What he was really interested in was why I had thrown the empty pint bottle of Old Overholt. And Murfin. He was interested in Murfin, too.

"These two guys with ski masks," Oxley said. "They both had guns, right?"

"Right."

"And one of the guys—"

"The one in the blue mask," I said.

"Yeah, the blue mask. Well, he goes into what you call the FBI crouch—"

"You know," I said, "like on television."

"Yeah," Oxley said, sighed, and perhaps even shuddered a little. "Like on television. Well, the guy in the blue mask has a gun and the one in the red mask has a gun, but that doesn't bother you any. You pick up an empty pint bottle and pop the guy with the blue mask on the arm with it just as he's about to shoot the Raines woman.''

"Obviously, Mr. Longmire was trying to prevent a cold-blooded murder," said Earl Inch, earning his $100 an hour. "I think he should be commended."

"Congratulations," Oxley said to me. "I think you're wonderful."

"Thank you."

"Now tell me again why you threw the bottle."

"I don't know," I said. "It seemed like a good idea. At the time."

"You didn't think that, well, maybe these two guys with the guns might get just a little offended? You know a little pissed off at you and maybe even get it into their heads that they oughta plunk a few shots your way?"

"Mr. Longmire was obviously willing to risk his life in order to save that of another," Inch said and sounded as if he almost believed it.

"Mr. Inch," Oxley said. "I know you're here to represent your client and all of us really appreciate your efforts. We really do. Honestly. But when I ask Mr. Longmire here a question I'd appreciate it if you'd just let him answer it and then, if you don't like his answers, well, you can sort of patch them up afterwards and tell me what it was that he really meant to say. Okay?"

Inch smiled. It was a cool, smooth smile that exuded the kind of confidence that comes from having an ego that's in tip-top shape. "We'll see how it works out," he said, committing himself to nothing.

Detective Oxley sighed again. "Okay, Mr. Longmire, tell me what you really thought about when you picked up that bottle and threw it."

"Nothing."

"Nothing?"

"If I'd thought about anything, I wouldn't have thrown it. If I'd thought that I might get shot, I certainly wouldn't have thrown it."

"Why didn't you think you'd get shot?" Oxley said, springing his trap if, indeed, that's what it was.

"I didn't think that I would or I wouldn't. I didn't think about anything. I just threw it and when the man in the blue mask pointed his gun at me, I wished that I hadn't."

Oxley leaned back in his chair staring at me with his icy blue eyes that looked as if they had been lied to a lot, but were finally getting used to it. He and Inch were about the same age, in their early thirties. Oxley wasn't too tall and carried enough weight around to make him seem almost dumpy. Inch, on the other hand, was well over six feet tall, lean, carefully barbered, or more accurately, coiffed, and had the smooth, fluid movements of a trained athlete, perhaps a tennis pro, which was a profession that he had once given serious consideration.

We sat there in silence for a while, Oxley glum and almost brooding, Inch serene and apparently delighted, although with what, I couldn't tell. Oxley ran a hand through his longish thin hair that was the nothing colour of old chewing gum, gave his holstered .38 a tug to make it ride more comfortably on his hip, and then took a sheaf of notes from his desk drawer, placed them carefully in front of him, and gave them a significant tap with his forefinger.

"That's quite a story you told us, Mr. Longmire, about how you got yourself involved in the Arch Mix disappearance and your sister and everything."

"I think I've told you all I know," I said.

"Yeah, we got that all down on tape," he said. "These here are some notes that another officer took down from what Mr. Murfin had to tell us. You happen to know what Mr. Murfin used to do before he went with the Vullo Foundation?"

"He was involved in a number of political campaigns."

"And before that?"

"He worked for a couple of labour unions."

"And before that."

"I think he was in the entertainment business."

"He never was a cop, huh?"

"Not that I know of."

"Tell me again how you'd describe the two men in the ski masks."

"Well, they were a little over average height, about average weight, and they moved as if they were in pretty good shape so I'd say that they weren't too old."

"What were they wearing?"

"Ski masks. A blue one and a red one."

"Besides that?"

I shook my head. "I really don't remember."

"Let me read you how Mr. Murfin remembers them," Oxley said. He started reading from the notes in front of him. " 'Witness said that perpetrator in red ski mask was a male Caucasian, five feet ten or ten and a half, weighing approximately a hundred and sixty-five or a hundred and seventy pounds, wearing long-sleeved blue sports shirt buttoned to throat. Witness further states that person in red ski mask wore pre-faded blue jeans with flared bottoms. Shoes, according to witness, were white Converse sneakers with three red slanting stripes. Witness not positive whether socks were black or dark blue. Thinks black. Weapon employed by person in red ski mask, according to witness, was thirty-eight calibre revolver with six-inch barrel. Witness is of opinion that revolver was S and W.' " Oxley looked up at me. "S and W," he said. "That's Smith and Wesson."

"I see," I said.

"It gets better," Oxley said and went back to his reading. " 'Witness states that perpetrator in blue ski mask was also male Caucasian, six feet tall, possibly six feet and one-half inch, weighing approximately a hundred and fifty or a hundred and fifty-five pounds, wiry build. Person in blue ski mask, according to witness, wore dark green, long-sleeved sport shirt, buttoned to throat, light tan corduroy slacks, flared bottoms, Levi brand.' "

Oxley looked up at me. "You wanta know the reason why he says he knew they were Levi's?"

"Why?"

"Because when the guy turned around Murfin saw that little red tab on the back that all Levi's have."

Oxley shook his head as if able to appreciate a true marvel when he ran across it and went back to his reading. " 'Shoes, according to witness, were crepe-soled desert boots, probably Clark brand. High tops made it impossible for witness to specify colour of perpetrator's socks.' "

Oxley stopped reading and looked up at Inch and me.

"It goes on for a little while more but you get the idea," he said.

"Mr. Murfin seems to have a true eye for detail," Inch said.

Oxley shook his head again, a little tiredly this time. "I've been in this business twelve years now and I never heard of any witness who apologized for not being able to tell you the colour of the socks of some guy who's pointing a gun at him."

"You should see him count a hall full of people," I said.

"Good?"

"Better than good," I said. "He's perfect."

This time there was a kind of weary disbelief in the shake that Oxley gave his head. "And you're sure he's never been a cop?"

"Not to my knowledge."

"Well, he certainly was helpful."

"That's good to hear."

"He even came up with a clue. At least that's what he said it was, so maybe it is."

"An important one?"

"How the fuck should I know if it's important? But just in case we might miss something, Murfin went up to the room that the Raines woman had rented and sort of poked around before we got there. You know, just to make sure that we wouldn't overlook anything. Well, he comes up with this clue of his." Oxley looked at me. "What does Chad mean to you besides being a country in west central Africa and a man's first name?"

"Nothing," I said.

"Nothing at all?"

"That's right," I said. "Nothing at all."

*   *   *

They let both Murfin and me go after I told them one more time about the man with the caterpillar eyebrows who I had seen coming down the stairs from Max Quane's apartment just as I was going up. It had happened the day before, but as I told it again it seemed as though it had happened last year. Early last year.

Afterwards Murfin, Inch and I had a drink in a small bar not too far from police headquarters. I let Inch buy because he probably was still charging me $100 an hour for the privilege of drinking in his company. While we waited for the drinks I excused myself and went back to the rear of the bar where the pay phone was.

The phone rang three times before Slick answered. After he said hello I said, "Sally Raines was shot to death this afternoon. I saw it happen."

There was a pause and then Slick said, "I see." Then he said, "I'm sorry," but that was only a mechanical response because Slick had known Sally Raines only slightly. "Is Audrey all right?" he said and this time there was real concern in his voice.

"She and the kids have gone out to the farm."

"Good. Can you tell me about the Raines woman—how it happened?"

I told him and when I was finished I said, "Slick?"

"Yes?"

"This whole thing is getting too close to home—to family. I'm worried about Audrey. She apparently told Sally something that Arch Mix had told her. Sally told Max Quane. Max is dead and so is Sally."

"But Audrey doesn't know what it is that she told Sally?"

"Not yet. But she might remember. Sally wasn't supposed to know what Max was up to either, but she must have put it together. Sally was smart. Very smart. Well, Audrey's not exactly dumb either so whoever killed Max and Sally just might decide to make it a clean sweep."

"Yes," Slick said, "I follow your reasoning. It's quite logical."

"Let's take my logic a step further," I said. "You told me there's a chance, a tiny one, I think you said, that Arch Mix is still alive."

"Yes."

"If Mix shows up, he can clear up this whole mess, can't he?"

"So I should think."

"All right, Slick, when?"

I could hear him sigh over the phone. "I really shouldn't have told you, dear boy."

"But you did."

"Yes, I did." There was another silence and then he said, "Forty-eight hours, Harvey. We should know within forty-eight hours whether he's alive. But I must caution you—no, I'm going to warn you—that if you mention this to anyone, you'll probably put Mix's life in grave jeopardy."

"You mean if he's alive, he's in real bad trouble? Or as you say, grave jeopardy, which sounds even more ominous."

"That's really all I can tell you."

"Okay, Slick. Forty-eight hours. If nothing happens by then, I'm going down to police headquarters and tell one Detective Aaron Oxley of homicide that you have certain information about Arch Mix that might lead to the solution of the murders of Max Quane and Sally Raines. You'll like Detective Oxley."

"If nothing happens in forty-eight hours, dear boy, I'll go calling on Detective Oxley myself."

14

Max Quane's house out in the Bannockburn section of
Bethesda, Maryland, was a block and a half off Wilson
Boulevard. It was a medium-sized, wide-eaved, one-storey
house built of dark red used brick with a shake shingle roof.
Its front lawn was green and neatly mowed and there were
four or five tall elms that helped give the place a permanent,
steady look—as if it were occupied by a family whose
breadwinner was predestined to get his GS 14 by Christmas.

The overhead door of the two-car garage was up and the
garage itself was partly filled by a large Ford station wagon
that was two or three years old. The rest of the space was
taken up with the junk that people put in garages because
they can't think of anywhere else to put it.

Max Quane's car, a green Datsun 280-Z with a DC
licence plate that read LEASED, was parked in the driveway.
Max had always liked to compose his own licence plates
and usually he came up with ones that were rather witty—or
cynical—like Max himself.

I parked the pickup in the street and walked up to the
front door, making my way around two boy's bicycles. One
of the bikes was supported by its kick stand. The other was
lying on its side in the middle of the walk so that you'd be
sure to trip over it. I picked it up and put it on its stand.
Then I went up to the door and rang the bell.

Dorothy Quane opened the door. She had a drink in one hand, a cigarette in the other, and circles under her eyes. She looked at me for a moment and then said, "Well, it's you. His other friend. You were his friend, weren't you, Harvey?"

"Sure," I said. "I was his friend."

"So he had two after all," she said. "I was beginning to wonder."

"You want me to come in or leave?"

"I don't know," she said. "I'm thinking about it. I guess I want you to come in."

I went in and followed her into the living room. She turned and gestured with the cigarette for me to sit anywhere. I chose the couch. She stood for a moment, looking at me. She wore blue jeans and one of Max's white shirts with the sleeves rolled up and the tails out. I could tell it was Max's shirt because of the tab collar.

"You want a drink?" she said.

"If it's no trouble."

"It's not if you get it. It's in the kitchen. It's bourbon. Wild Turkey. Ten dollars a fifth. Max had expensive tastes."

"I know," I said and went back to the kitchen, found a glass and fixed a drink. There were no dirty dishes in the kitchen. No smeared glasses or plastic sacks of unemptied garbage. Everything was as neat and as tidy as it was in the living room. I remembered that Dorothy had always insisted on having things neat. It was one of her minor obsessions.

I went back into the living room and sat down on the couch again. "Where're the boys?" I said.

She gestured vaguely with her glass. "Out," she said. Then she looked at her watch. "It's nearly six so they should be home soon. They're out somewhere, with their friends, I guess. Kids always have friends, don't they?"

"Almost always," I said. "What happened to yours? You used to have a lot of friends, Dorothy."

She sat down in a green wing-backed chair that was one of a matched set that flanked the fireplace. She looked at me, almost staring. At thirty-five Dorothy Quane was still a striking woman with one of those finely boned faces that help keep the years away. She wore no lipstick, not even a touch, but then she had never worn any. Her dark grey eyes were clear and I wouldn't have known that she had been crying if it hadn't been for her nose. It was red and shiny at the tip and I remembered that it always got like that when she cried, which I also remembered was often on Sunday afternoons. Especially on wet, rainy Sunday afternoons.

The circles under her eyes didn't tell me anything because Dorothy Quane had always had circles under her eyes. They were one of the things that made her appear so striking. The circles almost looked as if they had been artfully painted there for effect and the effect that they had, at first glance, was hauntingly memorable.

Finally she quit staring at me, took a swallow of her drink, a drag on her cigarette, and blew the smoke out as she said, "You're right, I did have some friends once, didn't I?"

"A lot of them."

"They couldn't take Max. I had the kind of friends who couldn't take Max so they sort of drifted away. You and Murfin are about the only people who could take Max, but then you and Murfin aren't like my other friends, are you?"

"I try not to be," I said. Those friends of Dorothy's that I remembered had been rather high-minded people who seldom approved of Max or wanted anything to do with him. I think they thought he was wicked.

She took another swallow of her drink, another drag on her cigarette, and looked into the fireplace. "I'm going to kill myself, you know."

"Oh," I said. "When?"

"You don't believe me."

"Sure I do. I was just curious about your timing."

"I'm not sure yet. I guess after the funeral. It's not going to be much of a funeral. Murfin can't find any pallbearers. That's pretty fucking funny, isn't it? A thirty-eight-year-old man dies and he hasn't got six friends or even acquaintances who'll be his pallbearers. I think that's pretty fucking funny."

"After the funeral," I said, "and before you kill yourself,

why don't you come out to the farm and bring the boys and stay a while. Ruth'll be glad to see you. You always liked Ruth.''

She looked at me curiously. "You're serious, aren't you?"

"Sure."

"Did Ruth put you up to this?"

"No."

"I don't know," she said. "How long could we stay?"

"As long as you like," I said, hoping that it would be three days, a week at the most. "I put up a new swing that goes out over the pond. The boys will get a kick out of it."

Dorothy Quane ground her cigarette out in an ashtray. She kept on grinding it and smashing it even after it was out. "I don't know," she said. "Let me think about it."

"You don't have to think about it. Just come on out Saturday after the funeral."

"Could I kill myself out there?" She made herself smile. It was a very tiny one.

"Sure," I said. "Why not?"

She rose and came over and picked up my glass. "I'll get you a fresh drink," she said. "Water, isn't it?"

"Water."

When she returned with the drinks, she handed me mine, and sat back down in the green wing-backed chair. Again she turned her head to look into the cold, empty fireplace that looked as if it had been freshly scrubbed. It probably had. "Did you know her?"

"Who?"

"Don't play fucking dumb, Harvey. You know who I mean. The girl that Max was fucking. The nigger."

"She was a nice, bright girl, if that's any help, which it probably isn't."

She caught the tense that I had used and turned her head to stare at me. "Was," she said. "You said was."

"She's dead," I said. "She was shot to death this afternoon. Murfin and I were there. We saw it happen."

Dorothy Quane didn't say anything for quite some time. Then she said, "I'm sorry. I was trying to sort out how I

feel about it and I think I'm really very sorry. I called her
nigger, too, didn't I? That's not like me, is it? Not like little
Dorothy Quane, the raving radical of Bannockburn who
marched with Martin at Selma.''

"Forget it."

"Did her getting shot have something to do with Max and
what he was messed up in?''

"I think so."

"You know how much money Max left?''

"No."

"He left six hundred and fifty-three dollars and thirty-two
cents. That's what was in the bank. He had ninety-six
dollars on him when he was killed. And some change. The
police said they're going to turn that over to me eventually. I
told them I could use it now. When he died I had eighty-six
dollars in cash and that went for groceries. Murfin said that
there's a cheque due from the Vullo Foundation. Max's last
paycheque. That'll be about twelve hundred after deduc-
tions. Maybe a little more. Max was making thirty-six
thousand a year plus a car and an expense account. It was a
good job, the best he ever had. But he spent it all. Or we
spent it all. He didn't have any insurance. I thought he had
insurance, but when I checked, he didn't. I don't know what
I'm going to do. I guess I'll kill myself.''

There are those who claim that there really isn't any such
thing as *déjà vu*, but suddenly I was back in the coach house
on Massachusetts Avenue and it was Sunday afternoon and
raining. I think I shuddered a little. Dorothy Quane went on
with her monologue, if that's what it was.

"I don't know what happened to Max. When I met him
he was a sweet, big-eyed kid who was going to help change
the whole world. You introduced us. We even talked about
joining the Peace Corps together. What a fucking laugh. The
only thing that Max ever changed was himself. He quit
being a sweet, big-eyed kid and made himself hard and
cynical and tough-minded. That was one of his favourite
words. Tough-minded. He found out he liked to manipulate
people. He was good at it. He manipulated me. I didn't
mind. I knew what he was doing. But other people didn't

like it and after a while they didn't like Max. I think they were afraid of him. He didn't seem to care. Politics suited him. It gave him a chance to manipulate people. After a while, that was about all he cared about. He didn't even care who he worked for. He even talked about working for Wallace once, but then Wallace got shot, and that fell through. He thought working for Wallace would be a joke. When I asked him who the joke would be on he said it would be on him. Max, I mean. Then he started going into these funny deals. I don't know what they were. He never told me. But one time he brought home ten thousand dollars in a paper sack and dumped it in my lap. He wouldn't tell me where he got it. He said it was just a deal he'd pulled off. He was always going to pull off a big deal. He was talking about it just before he got killed. It was going to be the biggest deal of all. He was going to retire at thirty-eight and we were going to take the kids and go to Europe. He seemed excited about it. We even went to bed together, which we hadn't done in God knows when. It was going to be a big, big deal. He was going to make two hundred thousand dollars, maybe more. Then he got killed and there wasn't any big deal. There was just Max dead and six hundred and fifty-three dollars and thirty-two cents in the bank. I'm going to kill myself, Harvey, I really am.''

She started to cry, but she did it silently and I remembered that she had never made any noise when she cried. I got up and went over to her and put my hand on her shoulder. She shuddered a little. It was what she did instead of sobbing. ''Come out to the farm Saturday,'' I said. ''Bring the boys and come out to the farm and we'll talk about how you're going to kill yourself. Maybe we can come up with something fairly pleasant.''

''You don't believe me,'' she said.

''I believe you.''

''No you don't.''

''Here,'' I said and handed her my handkerchief. She dried her eyes and looked up at me. ''When did you grow that?'' she said.

I gave my moustache a quick brush. "A couple of years ago."

"You know who it makes you look a little like?"

I sighed. "Who?"

"Don Ameche. You remember Don Ameche?"

"Sure," I said. "Don Ameche and Alice Faye."

"It makes you look a little like him except for those clothes of yours. What're you supposed to be?"

I glanced down at my clothes. I was wearing old faded jeans, which I thought were rather stylish, and a faded chambray work shirt that I'd bought from Sears before I quit buying things from Sears. "I'm not supposed to be anything," I said.

"You used to wear suits," she said. "I remember when you didn't wear anything but suits and vests. You even had them made in London. They were Savile Row, weren't they?"

"No, there was a place in Dover Street that made them."

"Max tried to dress like you used to, did you know that?"

"No, I didn't know that.'

"He's got thirty or forty suits and jackets in there. You and he were almost exactly the same size. If you want some of them, you can have them."

I thought about it. "I'll tell you what, Dorothy. I'll buy a couple of them."

"You can have them free."

"I'd rather buy them."

"Sort of contribution to the Widow Quane, right?"

"Why not?"

"Well, I can sure as hell use the money. Come on."

She rose, carrying her drink, and started back towards the bedroom. She had stopped crying. I followed her. The bedroom was as neat and immaculate as the rest of the house. Dorothy opened a large closet with sliding doors that took up most of one wall. She gestured with her drink. "Take your pick," she said.

There were about twenty-five or thirty suits and about fifteen jackets. They were all hung very carefully facing the same way on shaped wooden hangers. Most of the suits were hard-finished woollen worsteds, either blue or grey, although there were several nice tweeds and a couple of light summer-weight gabardines. Max apparently hadn't gone in for synthetic fibres. The jackets were mostly quiet tweeds or softly woven herringbone. There were also a couple of muted plaids. I decided on a light summer-weight grey worsted suit and a sporty-looking brown-tweed one that looked as if it had never been worn. I thought the tweed suit would go well in the country. It was rough and hairy and all I needed to go with it was a blackthorn walking stick. I also picked out a couple of jackets, a summer-weight one and a nice dark grey cashmere number. Max certainly hadn't stinted himself on clothes.

When I was through making my selection Dorothy Quane said, "You want to try them on?"

"No," I said, "I don't think so."

"While we're in here, you wouldn't want to go to bed, would you—just for old times' sake?" It was a casual, offhand, deadly serious invitation. Or proposition, I suppose.

"I'd like to, Dorothy, but I think we'd better not."

"Why?"

That was a good question and the only answer that I could give her that wouldn't make her threaten suicide or start crying again was a feeble one. "Maybe the boys might come home. You wouldn't like that, would you?"

"No, I guess I wouldn't."

"Maybe another time," I said brightly.

"Sure, Harvey. Another time."

Back in the living room she insisted that two hundred dollars would be a fair price for the suits and jackets, which new had probably cost at least eight hundred. Max had never bought anything but the very best, or the next thing to it.

I wrote out the cheque and handed it to Dorothy. "If you should need some more, let me know," I said.

She looked at me curiously. "You really liked Max, didn't you, even though nobody else did, except maybe Murfin?"

"He was a friend of mine."

"Do you still like me?"

I fought back a sigh. "I'm very fond of you, Dorothy. So is Ruth. We'll be expecting you out at the farm on Saturday. You and the boys."

"Maybe," she said.

"We'd really like you to come."

"Maybe I will," she said, "if I don't kill myself first."

15

It was a little after seven-thirty when I turned into the dirt lane that led from the road to the house. I stopped the pickup, switched off the engine, reached into the glove compartment, and took out a pair of binoculars. Through the glasses I could see them moving down to the garden. I counted three of them and recognized the one in the lead. He was a big, twelve-point buck deer, an old and valued acquaintance, the kind that a Texan might say of, "We've howdied, but we ain't shook." With him were two does. The deer were moving into the garden to eat my corn and grow fat. I didn't mind.

A lot of deer hung around the farm. They seemed to sense that nobody was going to take a shot at them. Sometimes they also came there to die after hunters had shot but only wounded them. When that happened Ruth tried to patch them up, if they would let her, and she had succeeded with four or five. But usually I had to finish them off with a surplus M-1 carbine that finally I had bought for just that purpose.

The deer weren't the only wild animals who thought of the garden as a free lunch. Besides the beavers there were raccoons, wild mink, squirrels, innumerable rabbits, and a swarm of muskrats that everyone told me I should trap, but which I didn't. The only thing I had ever killed, other than the wounded deer, was a twelve-button timber rattlesnake. There were also a couple of copperhead water moccasins that I might have taken a shot or two at if they hadn't moved so fast. I left the copperheads for the black snakes, the farmer's friend, who lived in our attic. At night we could hear them slithering around. Ruth and I found the sound rather comforting, but our infrequent guests said that it kept them awake.

I sat there in the pickup and rolled a cigarette and watched the sun start to go down behind White Rock on the ridge of the Short Hill Mountains. In the morning it would come up behind me over the Blue Ridge Mountains. The farm was in the very northwest tip of Virginia, in Loudoun County, only a mile or so from West Virginia and two miles across the Shenandoah River from Harpers Ferry. Directly in front of me, to the west and over the mountain, was the Potomac River and Maryland. If I got tired of one state, I could walk to another.

Sometimes when I turned into the farm I would stop and stare at it and wonder what impulse had made me buy it twelve years before. I was city born, city bred, and city oriented and even after a dozen years I still measured the farm in city terms: two blocks wide and maybe twelve blocks long, most of it straight uphill.

By trial and error I had turned myself into a pretty fair vegetable gardener and a so-so goatherd. But what I did best was grow Christmas trees. With the aid of the county agent, a proselytizer for the John Birch Society, and some additional advice from the Soil Conservation Service, I had eight years ago planted 11,000 white pines. Sentimentalists from as far away as Washington and Baltimore now came with their kids at Christmas to pick out and chop down their own trees. I furnished the axe. If they couldn't use an axe, they could use my chain saw. I charged five dollars a tree regardless of its size. But this year I was thinking of charging ten. After all, I had had to watch them grow.

As I sat there watching the sun go down I stopped thinking about Christmas trees and started thinking about what was really on my mind, which was the Vullo Founda-

tion and what I had come to regard as The Mysterious
Conspiracy Concerning Arch Mix. The area around Harpers
Ferry wasn't a bad place to think about conspiracies. It had
been the scene of a corker on October 16, 1859, when old
John Brown seized the federal armoury and then waited for
18,000 slaves in the area to join up with him in what he
hoped would be a big insurrection and just general hell-
raising. The only one problem was that Brown forgot to tell
any of the slaves that he was coming so none of them
showed up.

They sent Lee up from Washington to deal with Brown
and what was left of his ragtag band of twenty blacks and
whites, most of them under thirty and three of them not yet
twenty-one. Lee didn't even have time to change into
uniform. J. E. B. Stuart, plumed hat and all, talked Lee into
taking him along. Stuart was just a lieutenant then and
always ready for either a fight or a frolic.

A young marine lieutenant actually captured Brown. He
wounded him about the neck with a sword, but when he
tried to run him through with it the sword bent double. It
was a dress sword and not very sharp. Brown capitalized on
his wounds. When they tried him he lay on a pallet on the
courtroom floor. Most of the time he kept his eyes closed,
which was just as well because not too many could hold the
gaze of those fierce, strange grey eyes which nearly everyone said looked quite mad. Brown claimed that he wasn't
crazy, but then he lied a lot. He had an aunt who was crazy,
and two nieces and two nephews who had to be locked in an
asylum, so most folks thought it was hereditary. Brown said
if anyone should know if he were crazy, he should, and I'm
not, he said.

Crazy or not they hanged him in a field just outside of
Harpers Ferry. The field was surrounded by 1,500 soldiers
and one of the soldiers was Stonewall Jackson, although
nobody called him that yet, and another of them was young
John Wilkes Booth, then just a cadet, who would come to
know a considerable amount about conspiracy.

I quit thinking about Brown and Booth and their conspiracies, both of which had changed history, and went back to

The Mysterious Conspiracy Concerning Arch Mix. Mix had disappeared and so far no one knew what had happened to him. Two people who perhaps thought they knew had been killed. Furthermore, the labour union that Mix had headed was making some strange moves out in St. Louis and tomorrow I would fly out there to see if somehow that might have something to do with Mix's disappearance. Maybe it would all turn out to be part of some giant conspiracy. And then again, maybe it wouldn't, for if my Uncle Slick were right, there was a chance that Arch Mix was still alive.

I put my cigarette out in the ashtray, started the engine, and eased the car forward over the grave of The Proper Villain. There was a scream in the distance, and then another, but it was only Really Rotten Roger, the peacock, letting the world know that he had finally decided that it was okay for the sun to go down.

By the time I reached the house and parked the pickup it was twilight, although there would be plenty of light to see by for almost another hour. I picked up the neatly folded suits and jackets, the clothes that I had bought off a dead man's widow, and went around the house and climbed the steps to the porch.

Audrey and Ruth were sitting around the spool table drinking what seemed to be iced tea. Audrey looked drawn and a little pale. Her eyes were red-rimmed as if she had been crying, probably about Sally, I decided. After I said hello to both of them and told Audrey I was sorry about Sally, I plopped down into one of the canvas chairs, looked at Ruth, and said, "Get me a drink, woman."

"Tell him to get it himself," Audrey said.

Ruth smiled and when she did I was glad I was married to her and not to Audrey, although I was very fond of my sister in what has been described as my own peculiar way. "He's only teasing," Ruth said, rose, came over, and gave me a kiss on the head. She then looked at me searchingly for a moment and said, "It was really bad, wasn't it?"

"Godawful," I said.

"Where'd you get those?" she asked, noticing the suits and jackets that I was holding in my lap.

"I bought them off the Widow Quane who may or may not come to stay with us for a while on Saturday, if she doesn't decide to kill herself first."

"Is Dorothy very bad?"

"I've seen her better."

"I talked to the police," Audrey said. "After I got out here I called them and talked to a Detective Oxley. I talked to him for a long time about Sally. He told me what happened. He said you'd been down there, to police headquarters, you and Ward Murfin."

I nodded. "We were down there for quite a while. We told them what we saw. Oxley wasn't too much impressed with my description, but he thought Murfin's was superb."

"Sally didn't have to—well, I mean she didn't have to hurt for a long time, did she?" Audrey's voice broke a little when she asked.

"No," I said, "she didn't have to hurt. I think it was instantaneous or at least as instantaneous as death ever is." I saw no reason to tell Audrey about the cigarette burns that Detective Oxley said they had found on Sally Raines's body. Nor did I tell her about the gag that the police had found in the room that Sally had rented. I didn't really want to talk about Sally Raines any more or Arch Mix or Max Quane.

Ruth must have seen how I felt because she said, "What can I get you?"

I sighed, rose, and put the clothes down on the spool table. "Nothing, thanks, I've got to go milk the goats."

"They're already milked," Ruth said.

"You're a remarkable woman," I said and sat back down again.

"I had some help," she said.

"Who?"

"Your French-speaking niece and nephew. Their French is really quite good, especially Elizabeth's, although Nelson's is very good, too."

"Where are they now?"

"Still out with the goats."

"How did the kids take the news about Sally?" I said.

"Almost matter of factly," Audrey said. "Children are

often like that. Elizabeth was sombre and I suppose Nelson was grave. I was the one who broke down and cried all the way out here. I went on crying most of the afternoon. After that I talked to Ruth. That helped. I think the kids were worried about me.''

"And they're still out with the goats?" I said.

"I think they're trying to get them to speak French," Audrey said.

I smiled. "Maybe they'll succeed."

"Now that the goats are milked, what would you like to drink?" Ruth said.

"I think I'd like some gin," I said. "I think I'd like some gin and then I think I'll sit here and drink the gin and look at the fire-flies and listen to the frogs and the crickets. After that I'll have some dinner and then I'll take my wife to bed, if she's of a mind to."

"Be still my heart," Ruth said, batted her eyelashes at me, and then went into the house to fetch my gin.

Audrey and I sat in silence for a moment until she lit a cigarette and her paper match made a little popping noise. The slight breeze blew some of the smoke my way. It was marijuana. "You two really like each other, don't you?" she said.

"Yes."

"Do you know how lucky you are?"

"Yes," I said after a moment, "I think I do."

"Arch and I were like that," she said. "I mean I think we liked each other."

"Did he ever mention someone called Chad to you?" I said.

Audrey thought about it and then asked me how it was spelled. I spelled it for her. She shook her head and said, "No but he did talk about a Chaddi to me. I remember now because after I mentioned it to Sally she came back the next day and asked me about it again."

"Chaddi Jugo, right?" I said.

"That's right. He was president of one of those little countries down in South America, wasn't he?"

"Yes."

"Sally wanted to know everything that Arch had said about him. It really wasn't very much."

"What was it?"

"He just said that they were trying to do what they had done to Chaddi Jugo and he was going to stop them. That's all. The only reason I remembered the name was because it was so unusual. I asked Arch if Chaddi Jugo was Spanish and he said no, he was an American. Or had been born here anyway. Does it mean anything to you?"

"Maybe," I said, "but it probably would mean a lot more to somebody else we know."

"Who?"

"Slick," I said. "It should mean just a hell of a lot to Slick."

16

By noon the next day I was sitting in Ward Murfin's room in the St. Louis Hilton listening to him try to convince Freddie Koontz that we were no longer bastards, but really very nice guys. He was trying to do it by phone and Freddie didn't seem to be buying.

Freddie was the longtime director of the Public Employees Union's Council 21 in St. Louis who, according to Senator Corsing, had suddenly found himself out of a job. The Council, which virtually had been Freddie's life work, was composed of the dozen or so Public Employees Union locals in the St. Louis area. It served as their spokesman during negotiations, did the organizing, published their union newspaper, sometimes handled members' grievances, ran their credit union, furnished the locals with research material and even legal counsel, and most important of all, had provided Freddie Koontz with a rather nice livelihood for nearly twenty years.

"Freddie," Murfin was saying into the phone. "Freddie, goddamn it, will you just shut up and listen a second? I wanta make three points. First of all, the only reason Longmire and me are out here is that we'd like to find out what happened to Arch. Now that's one. Second is no, we're not working for Gallops. We don't like Gallops any more'n you do." Murfin stopped talking and started listen-

145

ing again. He listened for almost a minute before he broke in again. "Freddie, listen just a goddamned second, will you? Longmire isn't asshole buddies with Gallops. He doesn't like Gallops any better'n you do. That's right. Longmire's sitting right here in the room with me nodding his head up and down." Murfin started listening again but finally got the chance to break in with, "Look, Freddie, I know Longmire used to be a slick and slimy no-good son of a bitch. But he's changed. Christ, he even lives on a farm now. Can you imagine that? Longmire on a farm? Now listen, will you, and let me make my point, and then I'll shut up. If you'll just talk to us maybe it'll help us find out what really happened to Arch and maybe that'll help you get your job back. Just think about it." There was a pause and then Murfin said, "Okay. Okay. That'll be good. We'll meet you there at two."

He hung up the phone and turned towards me. "Freddie's got a long memory. He doesn't much care for us. Especially you."

"I don't blame him."

"But he's gonna meet us at a bar down near city hall at two. He says it'll at least get him out of the house."

I watched as Murfin rose, went over to his suitcase, and started unpacking. The first thing he unpacked was a fifth of Early Times bourbon that he set up on the dresser. I got up and went into the bathroom and came back with two glasses. I poured some of the bourbon into each glass and then went back into the bathroom and ran some cold water into the drinks. It was a kind of ritual that Murfin and I had observed when we travelled together. He brought the bourbon and I mixed the drinks.

I came back into the room just in time to see Murfin take the final item from his suitcase. It was a .38 revolver with a snub nose. A belly gun.

"What're you going to do with that?" I said.

"Put it under my shirts," he said.

"That's a good place," I said. "Nobody'd ever think of looking there."

"Last night," he said as he tucked the pistol away underneath his shirts. "Last night I got to thinking. Two people who were sort of mixed up with trying to find out what's happened to Arch Mix have got themselves killed. There was Max and then there was the Raines girl. I figured maybe if either one of them had had a gun, maybe they just wouldn't have got themselves killed. So I decided to bring a gun along."

"And put it away underneath your shirts where you can get to it real quick."

"Maybe I'll put it under my pillow tonight."

"That's a good place, too."

"You don't think I need it, huh?"

"I don't know," I said, "maybe you're right. I think that Max and Sally probably got themselves killed because they knew what Chad meant. I think I do, too, now. So maybe I should carry a gun around."

"You say you know what it means?"

"I think so."

"What?"

"When Sally wrote down Chad, I don't think she had time to finish. I think what she really wanted to write down was Chaddi Jugo."

I watched Murfin. His eyes glittered for a moment and then he smiled one of his more terrible smiles. I could almost see his mind working it out and sorting it over, moving the pieces around to see whether they'd fit. From the expression on his face he seemed to think that they fitted perfectly.

"Jesus," he said, still smiling as broadly and as nastily as I'd ever seen him smile, "it all goes together, doesn't it?"

"Yes," I said, "it all goes together."

* * *

The name of the bar and grill that Freddie Koontz had agreed to meet us in was called The Feathered Nest and it was the kind of place that was used as a hangout by those who had reason to hang around city hall. At two o'clock in the afternoon I thought I could spot three off-duty cops, a couple of lawyers, a bail bondsman, one pale man who looked hung over enough to be a reporter, and a pair of

rather pretty young women who seemed to be waiting for
somebody to buy them a drink. I had the feeling that almost
anybody might do.

It was a dimly lit place with a long bar. Opposite the bar
was a row of high-backed wooden booths. The rest of the
space was taken up by tables that were covered with the
traditional red and white checked cloths. The waiters were
elderly and morose-looking with seamed, dour faces that
may have got that way because their feet hurt. They wore
long, white aprons that almost reached their shoes.

One of them came back to the rear booth that Murfin and
I had chosen, flicked his napkin at our table, and said,
"We're outa the lamb stew."

"That's too bad," Murfin said. "We'll just take a couple
of draft beers."

"You coulda told me that when you came in and I
would'na had to walk all the way back here."

"Maybe you oughta think about buying yourself a skate
board."

"You wanta hear a poem?" the old waiter said.

"Not especially."

"It goes like this: two beers for two queers, a split-tail bass
for a country lass, and if that don't rhyme you can kiss my ass.
I don't remember the rest of it, but the sentiment's nice."

He wandered off and Murfin said, "This place hasn't
changed in fifteen years. They keep these old guys on and
encourage 'em to insult the customers because everybody
seems to like it."

"Atmosphere," I said.

"Yeah," Murfin said. "Atmosphere."

I was sitting with my back to the entrance of the bar and
couldn't see Freddie Koontz when he came in. But Murfin
spotted him and waved to let him know where we were.

When Koontz arrived at our booth he didn't sit down for
a moment or two but instead remained standing as he looked
first at Murfin, then at me, then back at Murfin again. He
didn't much approve of what he saw.

"You're getting fat," he told Murfin. "Longmire here
ain't changed much though. He still looks like a East St.

Louis pimp with a hard run of luck. That cocksucker moustache he's got now don't help none either."

"It's nice to see you, too, Freddie," Murfin said.

"Move over," Koontz said. "I don't wanta sit next to Longmire on account of I don't wanta catch something."

"Your mother still in the whorehouse business, Freddie?" I said.

"Nah, she quit after she caught the clap off your old man."

The insults were offered routinely and replied to in the same fashion, almost mechanically, without heat or rancour. It was simply what Freddie Koontz had long ago decided should be the proper form of address to go with robust male companionship. If you couldn't match him insult for insult, you were probably a pansy or worse, although it was doubtful that Freddie could think of anything worse.

Koontz had been born on an Arkansas farm nearly fifty years ago and there was still something bucolic about the way he looked even after nearly thirty-five years in St. Louis. He had a big head topped with a shock of greying hair that hung down into his robin's-egg blue eyes that were as innocent as evening prayer until he narrowed them so that they looked crafty and sly and maybe even mean. He had a large Roman nose, a wide, thin, sour mouth, and a heavy, jutting chin that made him look stubborn, which he was. He was also a big man, well over six feet tall, with thick, heavy, hairy wrists that stuck out from the sleeves of his expensive-looking grey leisure suit.

The old waiter came with our beers and grumbled when Koontz ordered one for himself. Koontz grumbled back at him, but he did it without any apparent pleasure. Instead, he kept peering around the back of the booth towards the bar. When his beer arrived he took a swallow of it, wiped his mouth with the back of a big hand, and turned to look at Murfin.

"Maybe you'd better tell me again what you and Longmire are up to."

Murfin told him and when he was through Koontz looked at me and said, "How come they picked you?"

"They thought I knew Arch as well as anybody."

He thought about that, nodded, and said, "You ain't been farming ever since '64, have you?"

"No."

"Longmire turned himself into a hotshot campaign manager," Murfin said. "I'm surprised you didn't know."

"Well, I ain't exactly followed his career, but if I'd had to make a prediction back in '64, I might've said he'd turn out to be a pretty good chicken thief. Or something like that."

Murfin took a sip of his beer and said, "How'd you ever let yourself get dumped?"

"How?" Koontz said. He seemed to think about the question for a moment and to help him think he looked up at the ceiling. "I reckon I got blind-sided. After Arch disappeared, I reckon it was only a couple of days after that, well, I get a call from Gallops, who was already playing chief nigger. Gallops says he's sending me out some help from Washington. I tell him I don't need any help. He says he's sending 'em out anyway. Well, we're right in the middle of negotiations for a new contract. We're not asking the city for much this time, just a touch here and there, and I've already sort of worked things out with the boys, if you know what I mean."

"We know," Murfin said.

"Well, the first thing I know these six guys that I never heard of before fly out from Washington. But they don't come near me. So the next thing I know there's this special meeting of the Council's board of directors and here're these six guys sitting there, not up to the table, you know, but back up against the wall. They all look alike. Maybe thirty or thirty-three, smooth-looking jaspers with real nice suits and shiny shoes. And from what I hear each of 'em's carrying enough cash money to burn a wet mule. So they bought it. The vote, I mean. There was a motion to dispense with my services, it was seconded, there's this six to five vote, and I'm outa my fuckin' job just two months before I'm eligible for a pension. Well, I start nosing around and I find out that these guys laid out about twenty thousand dollars cash money to rig the vote on the board of directors. I can't prove it, but that's what I hear and it adds up because the next time I see old Sammy Noolan—you remember old Sammy who never had a pot to piss in or a window to throw it out of either—well, Sammy's driving a Pontiac GTO and he never drove nothing better'n a second-hand Ford in all his life.''

Koontz took another swallow of his beer. ''Okay, so I'm outa my job, but I still keep in touch. Well, the next thing you know, the Council breaks off negotiations with the city. Wham! Just like that. Then these six guys that Gallops sends out from Washington come up with a new set of proposals. Well, one of the guys on the Council board, maybe you remember him, Ted Greenleaf?''

Murfin nodded to show that he remembered Ted Greenleaf.

''Well, Greenleaf's been around a long time and he takes one look at what these guys have come up with and he says to 'em that they're fuckin' crazy. Now Greenleaf's the one who led the fight for me in the Council meeting, although it wasn't much of a fight, so they don't even try to buy him off. They don't even try to argue with him. They just smile politely at him and let him have his say and on the way home that night his car is forced over the kerb and somebody beats the shit out of Ted Greenleaf and the next day he resigns from the Council board and puts it in writing. He has to put it in writing on account of he's in the hospital with his fuckin' jaws wired shut. You gettin' the picture?''

''Yeah, I think so,'' Murfin said.

''What do the new demands ask for?'' I said.

''Well, lemme tell you about that. That's really something. These demands ask for a whole passel of stuff but the key points are real simple. They're demanding a flat twenty per cent pay increase across the board and a four-day week. Well, I mean that sits with the city like a saddle on a sow. The city just laughs at 'em. But these six guys who've taken over the negotiations by now, they don't laugh back. They just smile as cool as you please and don't budge an inch.''

''What about the membership?'' Murfin said.

Koontz shrugged. ''Well, you know what the membership

is like. You tell 'em that they can have Friday or maybe Monday off as well as Saturday and Sunday plus a twenty per cent pay hike and, hell, they ain't gonna say no.''

"Yeah, but will they go out on strike for it?'' Murfin said.

"We used to put the Council newspaper out once every month, right?''

Murfin nodded. "Right."

"Well, now it's coming out every week and I mean it's slick. It's full of figures and statistics to show how the city can pay for all this stuff with no sweat. On top of that each member has received an individually robotyped letter explaining to him just how much money he'll make over the next five years when the city meets his demands. Well, shit, I mean it looks like a whole wad of money. All he has to do to get it is go out on strike for maybe a month or two. And even with what he'll lose in pay, he'll still come out way ahead, according to the phony figures that these six sharpers have come up with.''

Murfin shook his head. "The city'll never go for it. Hell, there's hardly a city in the country that's not almost flat-ass broke. They sure as shit won't go for any four-day week and a twenty per cent pay increase.''

"You ain't exactly telling me anything new,'' Koontz said. "But that's what they're gonna go for anyhow. After they dumped me they dipped down into the rank and file and came up with this loudmouth nigger who they made executive director. The second thing they did after they named him was to vote him a new Cadillac. Not a little Cadillac, but a big fuckin' Cadillac. Well, he gets his picture in the papers and on TV and they give him my salary and my expense account, and shit, there's nothing that nigger ain't gonna do for them.''

Murfin drank some of his beer and looked carefully at Koontz. "But you haven't just been sitting around the house all this time, have you, Freddie?''

Koontz took another look around the back of the booth towards the bar. Then he turned back, hunched forward, and lowered his voice to a hoarse, confidential whisper. "Well,

I've been talking to some of the guys and we're gonna have a meeting tonight.''

"Where?"

"At the fuckin' Odd Fellows Hall, can you imagine? Ten years ago I got the membership to vote that we oughta have our own headquarters. So they gave me the okay and I built us a hell of a fine place. Two storeys, nice big meeting hall, even a recreation room and plenty of office space. Even had a nice little wet bar in my office. Well, day before yesterday, I tell 'em I wanta use the union meeting hall and they lie to me and tell me it's all booked up. So I gotta go rent the goddamn Odd Fellows Hall for fifty dollars. Hell, I don't mind the money. I've paid more'n that to watch two flies fuck. It's the principle of the thing.''

"When's the meeting?" I said.

"At eight o'clock tonight. Some of the guys who ain't got just shit, clabber or mud for brains are gonna be there. They don't like all this strike talk either. Hell, if it was gonna come to a strike, we'd go for compulsory arbitration first. That's what Arch always said and I agree with him. Nobody knows how a strike's gonna turn out. For all you know it might bust the union and the first thing you know you'd be signing a yellow-dog contract to keep your job. You know, sign something where you'd agree to get out of the union if you're in it or not join it if you're not.''

"You think that's a possibility?" I said.

Koontz shrugged. "Who the hell knows?" he said. "You get a long strike and who's gonna get pissed off most? Well, the fuckin' voters, that's who, and they're already screamin' about how the city's got too many people on the payroll anyhow. Well, if a strike keeps them from getting their garbage picked up for two months, then come election day they're sure as shit stinks gonna vote for somebody who ain't gonna play patty-cake with no union. And don't think the pols don't know this.''

"Have you been talking to some of them?" Murfin said.

Koontz nodded glumly. "Yeah, I've been talking to them. Or they been talking to me, although they sorta sneak around to do it now that I'm out of a job. They're worried that if there's a strike, the party's gonna lose St. Louis and if it loses St. Louis, it's gonna lose the whole state. Well, that started me thinkin'."

"About what?" I said.

"I started thinkin', 'How come Gallops picked on me?' I mean, shit, I'm not the only frog in the pond. So I make a couple of long distance calls. Like I said, I ain't got nothing else to do. I call Jimmy Horsely over in Philadelphia and Buck McCreight up in Boston. I figure maybe they might have a spot for me. But whaddya know, they're just about to call me because the same thing's happened to them just like it happened to me. They got dumped and they're looking for jobs. And they tell me it ain't no use callin' Phil Leonard in New York or Sid Gersham out in L.A. or Jack Childers up in Chicago because they're dumped, too, just like I was, except Gallops sent in more guys and spent a hell of a lot more money to get the job done in those places than he did here. Whaddya think of that?"

Murfin looked at me with a glance full of something, significance probably, and then looked back at Koontz. "How about Detroit?" he said.

"Same thing," Koontz said. "Baltimore and Cleveland, too."

"Milwaukee?" I said.

"Same thing. Also Minneapolis and St. Paul."

"They're talking strike in all those places?" Murfin asked.

"That's all they're talking."

"Well," Murfin said, "ain't that fuckin' interesting?"

"Ain't it though?" Koontz said.

"You know what you just named, don't you?" I said.

"Sure I do," Koontz said. "I just named the ten or twelve biggest goddamned cities in the country."

17

Murfin was on the phone for nearly two hours before he finally hung up, turned to me, and held out his empty glass. I took it, poured some bourbon into it, and then filled it with water from the bathroom tap. When I came back, Murfin looked up from the notes he had been making, reached for his drink, and took an appreciative swallow.

"It all checks out," he said.

"I know," I said. "I was listening."

"I think we could use a few more details though. We'll go to this meeting tonight and then I think I'll take the long way back tomorrow."

"Chicago?"

"Chicago, Philadelphia, New York, and probably Baltimore. I'll land at Friendship and rent a car. A few more details won't hurt." He studied his notes for a moment. "How come nobody's put all this together before?"

"You mean the papers?"

"Yeah, the papers or maybe TV."

"Well, first of all it's never happened before so nobody's expecting it, and second, they don't have anyone to remind them of Chaddi Jugo."

Murfin nodded. "It all goes back to Hundermark, doesn't it."

"To him and the CIA."

155

"They brought you in, didn't they, back in '64?"

"Except that I didn't know it at the time. They wanted to make sure Hundermark got re-elected because if he didn't, they'd lose their pipeline into the Public Workers International. And they were right."

"It made quite a stink, didn't it?" Murfin said. "All about how the CIA was footing the bill for the PWI. It was Hundermark's pet project. He got some good trips out of it—London, Hong Kong, Tokyo—all over. I thought it was one big bore."

"It wasn't after Mix found out about it," I said.

"Yeah, first he fired you, then he blasted the PWI, and then he fired me."

"I'd already quit."

"Sure," Murfin said. "Who'd they send down there, the guy from Texas?"

I nodded. "Joe Dawkins. From Kilgore."

"He seemed like a hell of a nice guy. I wonder whatever happened to him."

"You mean after he dumped Chaddi Jugo?"

"Yeah."

"Last I heard he was doing good works for the CIA in Vietnam."

"Hell of a nice guy," Murfin said. "You ever talk to him about it? About Chaddi Jugo, I mean."

"Once. He got a little drunk and came over to my place. It was when I was still living in the coach house on Massachusetts."

"I always liked that place."

"Well, we talked about it just that once. I think Dawkins was trying to justify it. Chaddi Jugo was something of a Marxist, of course, who'd got himself elected president in 1962 of that former British colony on the east coast of South America."

"That didn't sit too well with the CIA," Murfin said.

"Chaddi wasn't just a Marxist, he was also from Chicago, but he'd somehow wound up down there and gone into politics and taken out citizenship. And right after Independence in 1962 he got himself elected president for a two-year term.''

"Yeah, but the British didn't like it."

"They didn't like it at all, according to Dawkins. They couldn't quite stomach having some Chicago Marxist being president of their former colony so they got together with the CIA to see whether there wasn't some way to dump Jugo in the 1964 election. Well, the CIA just happened to have its pipeline into the Public Workers International. It was into a lot of things back then—the National Students Association, a couple of magazines, and I think even a book publishing firm."

"Plus the Newspaper Guild," Murfin said.

"You're right. I'd forgotten. Well, anyway the CIA cleared it all with the AFL-CIO and it sent good old Joe Dawkins and God knows how much money down to South America to see what he could do about dumping Chaddi Jugo."

"And Dawkins pulled the strike," Murfin said. "It was a long one, I remember, but I don't remember just how long."

"Two months," I said. "It was the two months just before the election. Dawkins used his pot full of CIA money and his ties with the Public Workers International and somehow they struck everything—the buses, the railroad, the docks, the firemen, the police, the hospitals, and the whole damned government bureaucracy—even, or so Dawkins told me, the night-soil collectors. And most important of all Dawkins managed to make the blame for the strike land on Chaddi Jugo and stick to him. And that was about the last that anyone ever heard of Chaddi."

"What happened to him?" Murfin said.

"He got whipped."

"I mean after the election."

"I'm not sure."

"You know something?" Murfin said.

"What?"

"Max probably didn't have much more to go on than we do."

"And look what happened to him," I said. "All Max

probably needed to set him off was the mention of Chaddi Jugo's name and he got that from Sally Raines who got it from my sister. After that he must have made some phone calls just like you did and figured out why Arch Mix disappeared. Max's only problem was that he probably tried to cash in on what he found out.''

"How?"

"I don't know," I said, "but he told Dorothy that he had a big one going that might be worth two hundred thousand."

"That'd be a little rich for Max," Murfin said.

"That's what I thought. But apparently whoever he was trying to get the money from decided that he wasn't worth it, or didn't trust him, so they had him killed. I guess they had Sally Raines killed for about the same reason. She must have known what Max knew. I don't know whether she tried to cash in on it or not, but it doesn't much matter. She's just as dead either way."

Murfin took another swallow of his drink. "I figure the Arch Mix thing like this," he said. "I figure Arch somehow got wind of the whole deal and they had to take him out, right?"

"Probably. I know he'd never have gone along with it."

"No," said Murfin, "he wouldn't've." He was silent for a moment and then his face broke into one of his dirty smiles. "Jesus, it's sweet though, isn't it? You got a labour union to strike the public employees in ten or twelve of the biggest cities in the country just two months before election. Now who's gonna benefit from that?"

"Not the Democrats," I said.

"Not fuckin' likely. If they don't carry the big cities, then they don't carry the big states, and if they don't carry New York, Illinois, California, Pennsylvania, and at least couple of others, they're fuckin' dead come November second, right?"

"Uh-huh."

Murfin wagged his head from side to side in sheer admiration. "It's sure a sweetheart, isn't it?" Suddenly something seemed to bother him because his mouth went down at the corners and he wrinkled his forehead. "What I can't figure out is who the hell's steering it? It's not Gallops all by himself. He couldn't put something like this together. Not Warner B-for-Baxter Gallops.''

"No," I said, "he probably couldn't."

"And it sure as shit couldn't be the fuckin' CIA again."

I shook my head. "No, it'd be a little rich even for them, especially just now."

"And the Republicans wouldn't wanta take a chance on something like this, not with Watergate still hanging over them."

"I don't think they'd do it even if they knew how, although if it works, they're going to be the principal beneficiaries."

"You got any ideas?" Murfin said.

"I don't, but I think I know somebody who might."

"Who?"

"My Uncle Slick."

"What's he got to do with it?"

"I'm not sure that he has anything to do with it, but he might have some interesting notions. Especially since dumping Chaddi Jugo was all his idea to begin with."

18

The International Order of Odd Fellows Hall was about six blocks from The Feathered Nest bar and grill in a not particularly fashionable section of downtown St. Louis.

It was a two-storey brick building with a flat front. Downstairs was the bar and card-gaming area and upstairs was the main hall, which was large enough to seat probably 500 persons if all the chairs were up, which they weren't. Only fifty or sixty folding chairs had been set up in five or six rows in front of the speaker's podium. The podium rested on a long table.

By the time Murfin and I arrived and took seats in the rear there were twenty or twenty-five union members in the room, about three quarters of them men. Freddie Koontz, still in his grey leisure suit, was behind the podium in earnest conversation with a small band of members. There was much vigorous headshaking and nodding and when he wanted to make a point, Freddie Koontz liked to use two fingers to drive it home into his listener's chest.

Most of the members had stopped in at the bar downstairs and bought bottles of beer which they sipped from as they sat waiting for the meeting to begin. When Murfin saw the beer he asked me if I wanted one. I told him yes and he went downstairs and returned with a couple of bottles of Falstaff.

We were drinking the beer and watching the members dribble into the meeting when the woman came through the door. Murfin dug me in the ribs with his elbow. "Remember her?" he said.

"Jesus," I said. "She's changed."

"She's just older."

"She sure as hell is."

The woman must have been forty-six and looked it, but when I had first met her, a dozen years before, she had been thirty-four and looked twenty-five. Or maybe twenty-eight. Her name was Hazie Harrison and in 1964 her vote at the forthcoming convention was considered to be worth a special trip to St. Louis. I had been the one who got to make the trip.

She had been blonde then and she was blonde now, but that was almost all that had stayed the same. In 1964 she had been slender and willowy, but now she was chubby, if not fat, and her once pretty face sagged at the jowls and wrinkled around her eyes.

She stood in the doorway to the hall and the drink she held in her hand was almost dark enough to be iced tea, although I was pretty sure that it wasn't tea, but nearly straight bourbon instead. I remembered that she had liked bourbon. She stood there in the doorway and looked about the room as if seeking someone to sit next to. Her gaze ran by Murfin and me, stopped, and backed up. She dug a pair of glasses out of her purse, put them on, and looked at us again. She smiled, put the glasses back in her purse, and started towards us.

"She saw you," Murfin said out of the corner of his mouth.

"It's you that she has the real memories of," I said.

When she reached us she said, "Well, well, well, well, and well. If it's not Harvey Longmire and Wardie Murfin."

Murfin and I were up by then and I said, "How are you, Hazie?" Murfin lied and said, "You're looking great."

"I look like shit," she said. "I thought you guys were dead, but apparently you aren't, although with Ward here it'd be sort of hard to tell on account of he wasn't too much of a fuck as I remember, at least not like you, Harvey.''

"You haven't changed, have you, Hazie," I said.

"Why should I?''

"No reason.''

She cocked her head to one side and ran an appraising eye over me. "You look a little older, Harvey, but that's about all except for that moustache. I think it's kinda cute.''

"Thanks.''

"Does it tickle down you know where?''

"My wife says it doesn't.''

"You're married, huh?''

"That's right.''

"You know how many times I been married now?''

"At last count it was two.''

"It's five now and I might make it six. I got this old guy lined up who thinks I give terrific head.''

"I'm sure you do," I said.

She giggled. "You oughta know." She looked at Murfin. "You, too, baby.''

"Best in St. Louis," Murfin said.

She nodded gravely and I could see that she was more than just a little drunk. "That's what I was, wasn't I? The best fuck in St. Louis. Guys used to come from all over—from Chicago, Denver, Omaha, all over—just to find out if it was true and every man jack of 'em told me it was.'' She looked at me and smiled and I saw that there was a lot more gold in her smile than there had been.

"You remember that time you flew all the way out from D.C. to romance me into splitting off from Freddie and Arch Mix and going with Hundermark at the convention?''

"I remember," I said.

"It was 1964, right?''

"Right.''

"We stayed up all night, didn't we?''

"All night.''

"Then the next morning we called Murfin here and got him up out of bed in Washington.''

"My wife liked that," Murfin said. "She liked it a lot.''

"Then at the convention," she said to Murfin, "you took over to make sure that I stayed in line."

"It was pure pleasure," Murfin said.

"And I did, too, didn't I," she said. "I told you I'd go with Hundermark and I did because I always do what I say I'm gonna do. I never go back on my word. Never."

"You're tops, Hazie," Murfin said.

"You guys back with the union?" she said and swayed a little.

"Not exactly," I said.

"They're talking about a strike. I don't want no fuckin' strike. Strikes are dumb."

"I couldn't agree with you more," Murfin said.

"I been with the tax assessor's office twenty-three years and we haven't had any fuckin' strike yet. But all you hear about now is strike."

"Maybe they won't have one," I said, just to be saying something.

"Well, I sure don't want one. All I wanta do is have a little fun." She winked at me and then at Murfin. "How about later, after the meeting, you guys gonna be busy?"

"We got to catch a plane, Hazie," I said.

"That's too bad. But if you change your plans, lemme know. I got a girl friend who's real neat."

"We'll let you know," Murfin said.

"Well, I guess I better go find a seat."

"Nice seeing you, Hazie," I said.

"Yeah," she said with a note of surprise, "it was sorta nice, wasn't it?"

*   *   *

Freddie Koontz liked to make speeches, probably because he was very good at it. The one that he was making to the forty or forty-five members of the Public Employees Union was full of dire warnings about how an unjustified strike would affect their economic future. He made it sound grim.

"Lemme tell you something," he said in his speech-making voice, which was a mild roar. "I'm not against us

public employees striking. I've walked as many picket lines
as any man or woman in this room. I've had my head split
open by goon squads and I thought it was worth it because it
helped build the union. But the strike they're talking about
now ain't gonna build your union, it's gonna bust it.''

"You tell 'em, Freddie!" It was a woman's voice, slurred
but loud, and I didn't have to look to know that it belonged
to Hazie Harrison. There's usually at lest one drunk at every
union meeting, and this was no exception.

"The city's in rotten shape," Freddie Koontz went on,
ignoring Hazie, "and it got that way because the politicians
who run it are dumb managers. You know that and I know it
and about the only people who don't know how dumb these
guys really are are the people who vote for them. Well,
lemme tell you something, certain ones of these politicians
ain't so dumb that they won't welcome a strike with open
arms. You wanta know why? I'll tell you why. Because then
they'll have themselves a whipping boy to blame all the
city's problems on, and that whipping boy is gonna be you,
the members of Council Twenty-one of the Public Employees Union, AFL-CIO.''

That got a splatter of applause and another strident called
from Hazie to, "Tell it like it is, Freddie!"

And Koontz did, or at least he told it as he thought it
was. He warned that a strike would lead to a voter reaction
at the polls which could set the union's organizational
efforts back thirty years. He spoke of increased workloads
because of layoffs by attrition and by firings. He counselled
the members that collective bargaining was their best bet,
and if the bargaining process broke down, they should
demand compulsory arbitration instead of a strike.

"Lemme tell you something about this here compulsory
arbitration," he said. "If we got a dispute with the city,
well, the city's gonna be just as scared of what might come
out of compulsory arbitration as we are. Shit, they don't
know what kind of a deal might come out of it. Maybe
they'd have to pay more than they would if they sat down
with us and hammered out a contract. And that fear of the
unknown is what we oughta count on. Because it'll drive the

city back to the bargaining table and make 'em work out a settlement that we can both live with.

"Now if that don't happen and we go on this strike that they're talking about, well, a lot of you people right here in this room aren't gonna have jobs to go back to when the strike's over. And the ones who do have jobs to go back to might be given a little piece of paper to sign. And you wanta know what that little piece of paper is gonna be? Well, I'll tell you. That little piece of paper is gonna be a yellow-dog contract and that'll be the end of your union because the city'll have you by the balls."

Koontz was just going into his peroration when the six men came in. They looked cool and hard and confident. They were almost young, mostly in their late twenties or early thirties, and they had a look-alike quality about them, probably because of the dark suits they wore.

They came in quietly and scattered themselves through the audience. Koontz went on with his speech until one of them called out, "Hey, Freddie, I think you're full of shit."

Koontz stopped his speech and stared at the man who sat in the third row. It wasn't the first time Freddie Koontz had been heckled.

"Well, maybe you oughta know, pal, because you sound like you got a mouth full of it."

"Hey, Freddie," another one of them called out, "is it true you and the mayor are still sleeping together?"

Freddie shifted his gaze to his new interrogator. "If I went in for boys, Rollo, I'd pick one with a real sweet little candy-ass like yours."

"Why don't you shut up and let Freddie talk?" This came from Hazie Harrison who was now on her feet, swaying a little, and glaring balefully at one of the hecklers who had taken a seat beside her. The heckler used his foot to turn over the empty chair. The chair fell in front of Hazie. She stumbled against it, lost her balance, and went down in a heap on the floor. It was a nasty fall and a murmur went through the crowd. One man said, "Why don't you guys knock it off?" but he said it weakly.

The hecklers started tipping over the empty chairs then.

Finally, one union member, a slim young black, rose and went up to the heckler who seemed to be the ringleader. The black said, "Look, all we're trying to do is hold a nice, peaceful meeting. If you wanta stay, you gotta behave."

The ringleader was about six feet tall with cold, wet blue eyes and short-cropped blond hair that was trying to curl itself into ringlets. He looked hard and well-muscled. He smiled once at the black and even from where I sat I could see that his teeth were white and shiny and even. The blond man said something to the black, but I couldn't hear what it was. Whatever it was made the black swing at him, but the black's blow didn't connect because the blond man ducked it easily. The blond man then smiled again and hit the black hard in the stomach. He hit him twice. The black went whoosh and then sank to his knees as he doubled over and clutched his stomach.

The blond man looked around the room and said, "Folks, I think this meeting's just about over, don't you?"

Murfin turned to look at me. I saw the question in his eyes and I nodded. Murfin got up and moved over to the blond man with the cold blue eyes who now was nudging the bent-over black with his toe. Murfin's right hand rested on his hip pocket.

"Excuse me, sir," Murfin said, "but I think these folks would sorta like to go on with their meeting."

"Who asked you?" the blond man said.

"Well, I guess what I'm saying is that I think you guys oughta leave." Murfin smiled just a little as he said it. I stood up and started towards Murfin, an empty bottle of Falstaff in my right hand.

The blond man looked Murfin up and down carefully. The five other hecklers moved quickly across the room and formed a half circle behind the blond man. I glanced at Freddie Koontz who still stood behind the podium. Freddie gave me a small, almost imperceptible nod.

"You think we ought to leave, huh?" the blond man said to Murfin.

"Yes, sir, I think you should," Murfin said and smiled his polite little smile again.

"Well, here's what I think," the blond man said and threw a hard left at Murfin's throat. Murfin did a small, almost tiny dance step, ducked a little, and the left sailed past his right ear. The blond man just had time to look a bit puzzled before Murfin's right hand came out of his hip pocket. In the hand was a woven leather blackjack. Murfin smashed the blackjack against the blond man's upper arm. The blond man howled and clutched the arm.

The five other hecklers started moving towards Murfin who stood, half crouched, waving the blackjack back and forth with his right hand, beckoning the hecklers on with his left. I cracked the bottle of Falstaff against the back of a folding metal chair. It shattered, leaving me with the top half of the bottle and some nicely jagged glass. A very wicked weapon. I moved up beside Murfin and let the hecklers look at the sharp, shiny edges of the jagged glass.

"You two," the blond man said to a couple of the hecklers. "Take out the guy with the blackjack." The blond man was still clutching his left arm. "You other guys take out the one with the bottle."

They started moving towards us carefully, but confidently, as if they had done this sort of thing often before. They probably had. They stopped suddenly at the sound of another bottle being smashed against a metal chair. Freddie Koontz appeared at my side, a broken beer bottle in his big right hand.

"Come on, you cocksuckers," Freddie said.

The five hecklers hesitated for a moment until the blond man said, "There's only three of them."

Out of the corner of my eye I saw a big, heavy-set man in his forties rise from his chair, hitch up his pants over his belly, and move to Murfin's side. "There's four of us now," the big man said.

Another man, frail-looking and grey-haired with glasses, got up, took out his spectacle case, put his glasses into it carefully, and then took up a position next to the big man with the belly. The frail-looking man didn't say anything.

After that another man got up and joined us and then

another and then seven or eight more until we outnumbered the hecklers more than two to one.

"Like I was saying," Murfin said to the blond man, "these folks would sorta like to get on with their meeting, so I think you'd better haul ass outa here."

The blond man didn't say anything. Instead he gazed coolly at the union members who almost formed a half circle around him and his five look-alikes. The blond man, still clutching his left arm, jerked his head towards the door. The five other hecklers started to back towards it, never taking their eyes from the union members until they were halfway across the room. The blond man went with them. Then he stopped and looked back at Murfin and then at me. "I think I'll remember you guys," he said.

"I think you will, too," Murfin said.

The blond man nodded thoughtfully, then turned, and followed the other five out of the room.

*   *   *

Murfin and Freddie Koontz and I had a final drink in The Feathered Nest bar and grill. Koontz hadn't tried to get the meeting going again. Instead, he had let the members stand around and tell each other what they had seen and what heroes they had been. After they finally got tired of that, they went home.

Koontz now sat with us in a booth staring morosely into his glass of vodka and tonic. "That gave 'em a little boost," he said finally, looking up at Murfin and me, "but it won't last. They'll get home and start thinking about it and wondering what might happen the next time if they're damn fools enough to stick their necks out like that. Or they'll start wondering about what might happen if a couple of those guys catch 'em somewheres by themselves." He shook his head. "Well, at least you guys saw for yourselves."

"Uh-huh," Murfin said. "We saw."

"Whaddya think?"

Murfin shrugged. "It don't take much more than six guys like that, especially if they've got plenty of money."

"They've got it," Koontz said.

"So what I think is that you're probably gonna have yourself a strike, if that's what those six guys want."

"It's sure as shit what they want," Koontz said. He looked at Murfin and me and then dropped his eyes to his drink again. "You guys couldn't see your way clear to sort of stick around, could you?" He said it without hope, as though he knew what our answer would be.

"I don't see how we could, do you, Harvey?" Murfin said.

"No," I said. "It's just not possible."

"I didn't think it would be," Koontz said. His face screwed itself up into what seemed to be a painful expression and his mouth worked a little as though he wanted to say something that would make him hurt. Finally, he got it out. "I wantcha to know I appreciate what you guys did tonight. I'm much obliged."

"Forget it, Freddie," Murfin said. "Hell, me and Harvey enjoyed it. It was almost like old times, wasn't it, Harvey?"

"Almost," I said.

19

I flew back to Dulles the next morning and called Ruth from a pay phone. After we asked each other how we were she said, "Everybody missed you."

"I was only gone a day."

"We still missed you."

"Who?"

"I, for one, and all the dogs and cats, especially Honest Tuan who's been disconsolate."

"He'll recover."

"Then there're the goats. They miss your firm but gentle touch. And so do I."

"We'll do something about that when I get home. How's Audrey?"

"Better, I think. She doesn't seem quite so morose. She seems more pensive than anything."

"She's probably smoking a new brand of dope."

"No, I don't think so. I think she's resolving a lot of things."

"You mean about Arch Mix?"

"About him—and about Sally Raines. And herself, too. She's said a couple of things that lead me to believe that she may be on the verge of discovering that Audrey isn't as bad as Audrey thought."

"Self-acceptance huh?"

"Don't knock it."

"I don't. Another ten years and I might have some myself."

"You have plenty. If you had any more, you'd be arrogant."

"Instead of the way I am, right? You know, genial, solicitous, and easy to get along with."

"Exactly."

"I sound perfect."

"You are," she said, "and popular, too. You had some phone calls this morning. Three, in fact."

"Who from?"

"Senator Corsing called again. Himself. He said it was quite important for you to call him."

"All right."

"Then Slick called."

"Okay."

"And Mr. Vullo. Or rather his secretary. He's most anxious for you to call him. You want the numbers?"

"I think I've got them all. I may have to go see one or two of them so I'm not sure when I'll be able to get home."

"Make it soon," she said.

After talking to Ruth I called Slick, but he wasn't home. His answering service said that he would be back by noon. I called the Senator's office and the sweet-voiced Jenny put me right through to him.

"You're back," Corsing said when he came on the phone. "Good. He wants to see you."

"Who's he?" I said.

"I keep forgetting, Harvey, that you're not exactly caught up in the great sweep of politics any more."

"Not exactly."

"Well, he still wants to see you. You know, our standard-bearer. The man who. Our next president."

"Oh," I said, "him."

"Uh-huh. Him."

"What's he want to see me about?"

"There've been some rumblings from the outback. What we were talking about the other day. He called me about it and I said that you were looking into it out in St. Louis and that you might be willing to fill him in on what you'd found out. Are you?"

"For free?"

"Harvey."

"What?"

"There's no need for me to remind you, is there, that now is the time for all good men to come to the aid of the party?"

"There's no need, but it doesn't mean I have to vote for him, does it?"

"Do you still vote? I didn't think you still did anything like that."

"I vote against. I voted against Nixon twice. I don't think I've voted *for* anyone since I voted for myself twenty years ago down in New Orleans. I won, too."

"You told me. Well, will you fill him in?"

"It'll be bad news."

"Then that won't be any different from what he's become accustomed to."

"Okay," I said. "When?"

"Right away?"

"All right. Where?"

"Why don't you come by here and pick me up. He's got a borrowed hidey-hole out in Cleveland Park that he thinks nobody knows about. They wouldn't either, if it weren't for the swarm of Secret Service and press types that have to dog him."

I looked at my watch. "I'm out at Dulles. I can pick you up outside in an hour."

"Fine. I'll call and tell him we'll be there in an hour and a half."

After Corsing hung up I called Roger Vullo's office and talked to his secretary who said Vullo was out, but had left a message. The message was that it was imperative that I see him at his office at two.

"Did he say imperative?" I said.

"Yes, sir. He was quite explicit about the phrasing," Vullo's secretary said.

"Tell him I'll be there at two-thirty."

*   *   *

Corsing was waiting for me on the steps of the Dirksen Senate Office Building but I had to honk four times and even wave a little before he could bring himself to believe that he was going to have a ride in a pickup.

When he climbed in I said, "What'd you expect, the Bentley?"

"No, just something with a back seat maybe." He looked around the cab of the pickup and said, "Where's your gun rack? I didn't think any of you hoot and holler West, by God, Virginia–type ridge runners would be caught dead in their pickups without a gun rack."

"I live in Virginia, not West Virginia. We're more sedate over there. More cultivated, too."

"Where'd I get the idea that your farm was in West Virginia?"

"Probably from my sly country ways."

"Probably," the Senator said. "Well, did you see Freddie Koontz?"

"I saw him."

"How was he?"

"Pissed off. Embittered. Dispirited. And perhaps a bit bemused by fate. He was just a few months away from his pension when they dumped him."

"Well, maybe I can find him something."

"I don't think he'll settle for something. He wants his old job back."

"Do you think he has a chance?"

I shook my head. "It doesn't look that way."

*   *   *

The hidey-hole that the man who wanted to be president had found for himself was a big, ugly, faintly Norman house down back of the Shoreham Hotel and just across the street from Rock Creek Park on Creek Drive. Corsing showed some identification proving that he was a U.S. senator to one of the Secret Service men who were hanging about outside and who, after giving the pickup a stare of disbelief, directed us to a place where we could park.

We had to make our way past a gaggle of newsmen, or persons, I suppose, since there were a couple of cold-eyed women among them. All of them knew the Senator and several of them knew me and it was easier to stop and lie to them than it was to brush them off.

Three reporters from the television networks stuck their microphones into Corsing's face. He stopped and the rest of the newsmen gathered around on the off chance that he would say something that they could record or write about.

The ABC reporter was first off the mark with, "Senator, some people say that this campaign is foundering. You've got a reputation of being one of the most astute politicians in the country. Are you here to help try to put the campaign back on the track?"

Corsing grinned and brushed back his floppy shock of greying hair. It was a familiar gesture, almost his trademark. He stopped grinning and tried to look grave and perhaps statesmanlike, but there was too much twinkle in his eyes to bring it off.

"First of all, I'd like to go on record here and now as being firmly opposed to mixed metaphors. If this campaign were foundering, which it certainly is not, one might man the pumps or throw out a towline, but one most assuredly would not put it back on the track. Actually, Mr. Longmire and I are here not to give advice, but for another highly important reason."

"What reason, Senator?" CBS asked.

"Lunch."

"Aw shit."

They made one more try, this time with me. "Hey, Harvey," the *Baltimore Sun* man asked, "are you being asked to jump into this thing?"

"Not that I know of."

"Would you, if you were asked?"

"I don't think so."

"Why not?"

"I'm trying to quit," I said.

"Who's he?" I heard a young female reporter ask one of the greybeards.

"Longmire. Harvey. He used to be a hotshot campaign manager."

"I think he's kinda cute," she said.

"He's married."

"Who gives a shit?"

Inside the house we were met by a pale young man who wore a slightly harassed expression plus the rather glazed look of someone who's trying to think of three dozen things at once. He probably was.

"This way, Senator, and Mr.—uh—Longmire, isn't it?"

"Longmire," I said.

"We'll go right in," he said, and started off down the centre hall that was lined with some highly polished antiques and a number of quite interesting paintings. I thought I spotted a Miró, but I wasn't sure.

"Who owns this place?" I asked Corsing as we followed the young man down the hall.

"It belongs to our former ambassador to Italy who very much hopes that he'll be our next ambassador to England."

"His wife's got the money, right?"

"Right."

The man who wanted to be president was seated in his shirt-sleeves behind a large carved desk in a book-lined room that must have been the library. "Hello, Bill," he said as he got up and stretched out his hand. The Senator shook it and turned towards me. "You know Harvey, of course."

"Harvey," the Candidate said, "it's good to see you again."

"My pleasure," I said.

"It's been a while, hasn't it?" he said. "Six years?"

"Eight, I think. In Chicago."

"Yeah," he said. "Chicago. Wasn't that a fucking mess."

"Wasn't it though."

The Candidate turned towards the pale young man who was scribbling something into a notebook. He scribbled furiously as if he were afraid that he would forget it before he got it written down. "Jack, have they delivered that lunch we ordered yet?"

"Yes, sir, it just got here."

"Can you have somebody serve it in here?"

"Right away," the young man said and turned to go.

"Wait a minute," the Candidate said. He looked at Corsing and me. "We've got a no-booze rule around here, but I think we could scare up a couple of bottles of beer seeing that it's August and the gentlemen look thirsty."

"A beer would be fine—since it's August," Corsing said.

"Harvey?" the Candidate said.

I nodded. "Sure."

He turned to the pale young man. "You got that, Jack?"

Jack nodded. "Two beers and one Tab," he said and left.

The Candidate gave his stomach a gentle whack. "I've got to keep it down." He moved over to a burnished oval table and said, "Let's sit down over here. We'll eat while we talk."

He sat at one end of the table and Corsing and I sat on either side of him. I took out my tin box and started to roll a cigarette. The Candidate got up, went over to his desk, and came back with an ashtray that he slid across the table to me. I thanked him.

"Okay," he said, "let me tell you what I've got and how I got it and then we'll see whether it fits in with what you guys have."

I nodded and so did Corsing.

"There's a very bright kid on our staff," the Candidate went on, "who's helping handle the labour side of things. About two or three weeks ago he started to get some strange reports—except that they didn't look strange at the time, not until he put them all together. Analysed them. Then he wrote up a report and tried to get it to me, but you know how campaigns work."

"Somebody shortstopped it," I said.

"Yeah. Not intentionally, but nevertheless it fell between the cracks somewhere. Well, I started getting a howl from here and a squeal from there and so I asked our guy who's supposedly our liaison with labour what the hell's going on. He fished the kid's report out from between the cracks, dusted it off, and tried to pass it off to me as being freshly written. Well, it looked grim, but what the hell, everything looks grim in a campaign like this. But something about the report bothered me so I asked to see the person who'd written it."

The Candidate ran a hand through his hair that had a lot more grey in it than it did eight years before. "Well, the kid comes in and despite the fact that nobody's encouraged him to, he's prepared an update on his previous report. And the update doesn't look grim, it looks like a blueprint for an unmitigated disaster. If the kid's information is right, the public employees of ten of the largest cities in the country will go on strike during the first week in September which I don't have to tell you is just two months away from November second, a date that's of some importance to me and mine. How's that jibe with what you've got, Harvey?"

"Pretty well," I said, "except that I think it's going to be twelve cities rather than ten."

"Christ," the Candidate said. "What's your source?"

"I just got back from St. Louis. There's going to be a strike in St. Louis unless I'm very much mistaken. They've locked themselves into their position and they won't budge. Or so I'm told."

"What do they want?"

"For starters, a four-day week. For dessert, a twenty per cent pay raise."

"What about elsewhere?" the Candidate asked me.

"There seems to be a pattern. After Arch Mix disappeared the union hired two hundred new guys and gave them International Organizers as their title."

"Two *hundred*?"

"Two hundred," I said. "They fanned out over the country and the first thing they did was dump the local union leadership in the dozen big cities that I mentioned. Money seems to be no problem. They bribed and bought where they had to and if that didn't work, they used muscle. From what I saw in St. Louis, they're a pretty mean bunch. Once they had the local leadership dumped, bribed or intimidated, they took over the negotiations. Except that they don't really want a settlement, they want a strike."

The Candidate nodded. "You're sure about the bribes and the muscle?"

"I'm positive about it in St. Louis. Somebody else is

checking it out in Chicago, Philadelphia, New York and probably Baltimore. He's due back tomorrow."

"Do I know him?"

"Uh-huh, you know him. It's Ward Murfin."

The Candidate started to say something else, but before he could the door opened and a young woman of about twenty-two came in carrying a large tray that was covered with a white cloth. Shepherding her across the room was Jack, the pale young man with the slightly glazed look.

She set the tray down on the table and then spread a white linen cloth. The Candidate, ever mindful of every vote, said, "How're you today, June?"

The young woman smiled and said, "Just fine, sir."

She served the two beers to Corsing and me and the Tab to the Candidate. Then she whisked away the cloth that covered the tray. Lunch, I saw, was going to consist of three McDonald Big Mac hamburgers. With french fries.

The Candidate served us himself. Then he took a big bite out of his hamburger. Once he was chewing properly June and Jack left. I took a swallow of beer.

Before taking another bite of his hamburger, the Candidate said, "I talked to Meany."

"What'd he say?" Corsing asked.

"He said it's a question of autonomy. That was on the record. Off the record, he said that the AFL-CIO's relations, meaning his, hadn't been too good with the PEU when Arch Mix was there and now that he's disappeared, they're even worse. He said that there wasn't anything he could do unless he received a specific complaint, which he hasn't, and even if he did he wasn't sure that he could do anything to keep them from going out."

"If he did anything, the PEU might take a walk," I said. "That would mean that the AFL-CIO would lose its fastest-growing union. Ninety thousand new members a year, the last I heard."

"That won't happen," the Candidate said. "Well, after I talked to Meany I got hold of one of our guys who used to have pretty good connections with the PEU. Excellent connections, in fact. So he went down to see this new guy that's taken over—the black guy—uh—''

"Gallops," I said.

"That's right, Gallops. Warner B. Gallops. Well, as I was saying, this guy who supposedly was in tight with the PEU went down to see Gallops to ask what the hell was going on and to point out that if they struck the ten biggest cities in the country, then I'm going to be stone cold dead on November second.''

"What'd Gallops say?" I said and took a bite of my hamburger. It was cold.

"Well, he said something and then he did something," the Candidate said. "First—and I think I'm quoting accurately now—he told my guy, 'It's none of your fucking business what we do,' and then he threw him out on his ass.''

"Literally?" Corsing asked.

"Close enough."

I took a bite of one of my french fries. It was cold, too. "You're in trouble," I said.

The Candidate nodded, put what was left of his Big Mac down, wiped his fingers on a paper napkin, and took a folded sheet of paper out of his shirt pocket. He unfolded it and put on a pair of glasses. I noticed that they were bifocals. "This is the latest poll," he said. "The private one. Right now we're running forty-six forty-four with twelve per cent undecided. I've got the forty-four. That means I'm up one per cent from last week. They say we're going to peak the last week in October. That'd be just about right wouldn't it, Harvey?"

"It would be perfect," I said.

"But if Gallops pulls off these strikes, we're not going to have to worry about peaking, are we?"

"No," I said, "if he does that you can start writing your concession speech. Maybe something witty and poignant like Stevenson had in '52."

The Candidate stuck a fistful of french fries into his mouth and chewed rapidly. He seemed hungry or maybe he found food a comfort and a solace. Many do. Still chewing, he looked at Corsing and then at me.

"I don't have to tell you what the reaction to these strikes would be, do I?" he said and then went on before we could say yes or no. "I don't have to describe how the voters feel about strikes by teachers and cops and garbage collectors and hospital workers and what have you. And I don't have to tell you what frame of mind the voters are going to be in on November second if they haven't had their garbage picked up in two months, or worse—much worse—maybe they've had a friend or relative die because there wasn't enough help to go around in a hospital. Or maybe their kid, or the neighbour's kid, got hit by a car at a school crossing because there wasn't anybody there to help him across the street because whoever was supposed to be there was out on strike. I don't have to tell you who they're going to vote for if something like that happens, do I?"

"No," I said, "you don't."

"I'll tell you anyhow," he said. "In the big cities they'll vote us out and them in."

"That's a safe prediction," Corsing said.

"Okay," the Candidate said, "who's back of it?"

"That's simple," I said. "Find out what happened to Arch Mix and you'll probably find who's back of it."

"The FBI isn't having much luck, is it?"

"Not much," I said. "None, in fact."

"You going to eat your french fries?" the Candidate said.

"No."

"Good." He reached over and took three or four and crammed them into his mouth. "Gallops must know," he said.

"Not necessarily," I said. "He may be just a tool."

"The unwitting kind?"

"Who know? Maybe somebody's paying him a little money. Or maybe he's just ambitious. Try this one on. Suppose Gallops came to you about September first and said, 'There won't be any strike if you put it in writing that you'll make me Secretary of Labour.' "

The Candidate didn't reject the idea out of hand. He thought about it first as he reached for the rest of my french fries. "I'll deny it if it ever gets out of this room, but if that were to be the price, I might agree to pay it."

"I don't blame you," I said. "But I don't think it's going to happen. I think somebody's steering Gallops."

"Them?" he asked.

"No," Corsing said. "They wouldn't do it. They're too busy trying to make everyone forget Watergate."

"If I didn't know better," the Candidate said, "I'd say that some of those nuts out at the CIA are up to their old tricks."

"How about the Mafia or whatever they're calling it nowadays?" I said.

The Candidate thought about it. "What's their angle?"

"Extortion," I said. "The cities will leave them alone to operate wide open in exchange for no strikes."

"Any proof?"

"None."

He shook his head. "Put it down to paranoia, if you want to, but I think the stakes are higher than that. I think they're playing for the presidency."

"Have you got any idea of who they might be?" I said.

He shook his head again. "None. Do you?"

"It's somebody with a lot of money," I said, "although they might not know how it's being spent. In fact, they might not want to know."

"That's cryptic," he said.

"It was meant to be."

"You've got an idea?"

"Possibly," I said, "but that's all it is."

"But there's a chance?"

"I'm not sure it's even that."

"Can you give me a hint?"

"No."

"Harvey?"

"Yes?"

"If whatever you're up to somehow prevents these strikes, I'll be grateful."

"I should hope so," I said.

"How'd you like to be White House press secretary?"

"Not very much," I said. "Not any at all, in fact."

20

After I dropped Senator Corsing off at his office I found a pay phone and called Slick. Once again I got his answering service who informed me that he now was expected to return around four. I looked at my watch and saw that it was one-forty. I thought a moment, then picked up the phone book and looked up a number. The number that I looked up belonged to Douglas Chanson, the headhunter. With much reluctance, he agreed to give me ten minutes at two o'clock.

If I had to go down to an office every morning, which is a recurring bad dream that I have about two or three times a month, I suppose I would prefer it to be like the one that Douglas Chanson had on Jefferson Place, a one-block street that runs between Eighteenth and Nineteenth just north of M Street.

It's a quiet block consisting mostly of narrow, brightly painted, three-storey townhouses with a number of trees and lots of small, highly polished brass plates that discreetly announce the names of those who do business there. There were quite a few lawyers on the block, but some of the brass plates simply gave a name with no indication of the profession that went with it, and I liked to think that these unnamed professions were mysterious and perhaps even a bit nefarious.

Douglas Chanson Associates had such a brass plate above

the doorbell of a three-storey townhouse that was painted a rich cream colour with black trim. I tried the door, but it was locked, so I rang the bell. There was an answering buzz and I went in and found myself in what probably used to be the foyer but was now a reception area presided over by a young, slim brown-haired woman with green eyes.

She looked at me and then her watch. "You'd be Mr. Longmire."

"That's right."

"You're early."

"To be early is to be on time," I said, a little sententiously.

"To be early means you'll have to wait a few minutes," she said. "Here. Fill this out." She moved a small form across her desk. I picked it up and read it. The form wanted my name, my spouse's name, my occupation, my business address, my home address, my business and home phones, and my Social Security number.

I put it back down on the desk. "The name is Harvey Longmire," I said. "And I'm not looking for a job."

"It doesn't matter," she said. "Mr. Chanson still likes the information for his records."

"My address is a post office box, my phone is unlisted, I don't remember my Social Security number, and this week my occupation is beekeeper."

She grinned at me. It was a saucy kind of grin. "We don't get much call for beekeepers. What do you really do?"

"For the record?"

"Just curiosity."

"As little as possible."

"Does it pay anything?"

"Not much."

"Enough to buy me a drink at the Embers at, say, five-thirty?"

"Why don't we make it at my place at six. You'll like my wife. Her name's Hecuba."

She grinned again. "Well, I tried." She picked up the phone and punched a button. "Mr. Longmire, the bee-keeper, is here." She listened and then she said, "He says he's a beekeeper, I don't." There was another pause and then she said, "All right," and hung up the phone. "Right through there," she said, indicating a pair of sliding double doors.

I started for them and she said, "Her name's not really Hecuba, is it?"

"Uh-huh," I said. "She was named after her Uncle Priam's first wife."

She was writing it all down on the form as I slid back the sliding doors and went in. What I entered wasn't an office or even a study. Rather, it was somebody's impression of what the number two reception room of a turn-of-the-century London club must have been like. There was a fireplace with a fire that crackled in August and for a moment I wondered why I wanted to go over and warm my hands in front of it until I realized that the temperature in the room had been brought down to about sixty or sixty-five degrees by air conditioning.

There was no desk in the room, just an oak library table against one dark-panelled wall. The drapes were of plum velvet and the carpet was a deep mauve colour. In front of the street windows were a couple of comfortable-looking wing-backed leather chairs with a small table in between them. The chairs would be nice to sit in after a good lunch and watch it rain on the pedestrians. There was also a couch or two in the room, one of which looked like it would be just right for an afternoon nap. Flanking the fireplace was a cane-backed settee and a deep leather armchair that a man was sitting in, an open grey file on his lap. He looked up at me, put the file down on a table that held a 1908-type telephone, and got up. He didn't offer to shake hands; instead he nodded at me, and gestured that I should sit on the settee.

He was about forty-five or fifty, I decided, although it was hard to tell because of the brown beard that was formed by the moustache that ran back down his cheeks to join his long sideburns, leaving his chin bare. I couldn't remember what that particular style of beard was called, but I remembered from old photographs that it had been popular during the latter part of Victoria's reign.

"Do sit down, Mr. Longmire," he said. His accent wasn't British, but it was still nicely clipped.

I sat down on the settee and looked at Douglas Chanson. He wore a dark, almost black suit with a dove-grey vest and a plain, wide, deep-purple tie. His glistening white shirt and collar looked stiff and starched. Above the stiff collar was an equally stiff face that didn't look as if it laughed much. The bare chin that poked out from the beard was bony and narrow and above it was a small pursed mouth. Above the mouth was a thin nose and a pair of shiny brown eyes and in between the eyes were lines of what seemed to be a perpetual vertical frown that creased the centre of his pale forehead. He combed his brown and grey hair carefully down over his forehead to make it look as though it wasn't as thin as it was. Douglas Chanson, I decided, had a generous amount of vanity.

He stared at me carefully for several moments and then said, "I don't usually do this and I wouldn't have in this instance unless you'd said that you were associated with Roger Vullo."

"You checked, I take it."

"Naturally."

"I'd like to ask some questions about one of your clients."

"I'm not at all sure that I'll answer them. I think you should understand that from the outset."

"I'd like to ask them anyway."

"All right."

"The client is the Public Employees Union."

"Yes."

"You recently recruited two hundred new employees for them, right?"

"Two hundred and three, actually."

"I'm curious about what qualifications they had to have. I recently ran into six of them out in St. Louis."

"St. Louis? Let's see, that would be Russ Mary and his team, I believe. Yes, Mary."

"A rather tall blond guy with cute little waves in his hair?"

"Mr. Mary is rather tall and blond but I don't find his hair cute."

"What's his background?"

''That's one of the questions that I choose not to answer.''

''Let me put it another way,'' I said.

''If you wish.''

''Mary doesn't have a labour organization background, does he? What I mean is, has he ever worked for another union other than the PEU?''

''No.''

''Has he ever worked for the federal government?''

''I'd have to say yes to that, but with certain qualifications which I'm afraid I can't mention. Do you smoke?''

''Yes.''

''Good. Perhaps you'd like one of my cigarettes.'' He picked up a small, highly polished wooden box that may have been made out of rosewood, opened it, and offered it to me. It contained long brown cigarettes. I took one. So did Chanson. He produced a gold lighter from a vest pocket and leaned forward to light my cigarette. Then he lit his own and leaned back in his chair, drew some smoke down into his lungs, and exhaled it. I took a puff of my own. It wasn't bad.

''I have them made for me in New York,'' he said. ''They contain no artificial preservatives. No saltpetre and what have you. I seem to like things that haven't been tampered with.''

''I roll my own,'' I said.

''Do you really. That's interesting.'' He said it as if it really were.

I took another drag on my cigarette and said, ''Having met Mary and his five helpers, I was wondering if the other hundred and ninety-seven persons that you recruited for the union were similar.''

''In what way?''

''Mary struck me as a rather take-charge type of guy. Competent. Aggressive even.''

''You mean tough as a boot.''

''Yes,'' I said, ''maybe I do mean that.''

''The team leaders that I chose are quite similar to Mr. Mary. The helpers as you call them are—how should I put it—competent, let's say, but in need of firm direction.''

"It must have been quite an assignment. Finding two hundred competent people to do anything can't be an easy task."

Chanson nodded judiciously. "But not as difficult as one might think providing you have the resources and enough lead time."

"You didn't have very much, did you? Lead time, I mean."

"Actually, we had quite a bit although it may not sound like much to you."

"How much?"

"Nearly a week."

"That's all?"

"Sometimes we're only given a day or two."

"Who approached you?"

"From the union?"

"Yes."

"That's another question I choose to skirt, Mr. Longmire. I can only say that the initial approach was made by a confidential emissary from the union. Let me explain my secretiveness so you won't think that I'm being overly arcane and mysterious. You see, in my business we often have corporate, organizational, and even government clients who decide to make sweeping changes from top to bottom. Replacing these personnel quickly is a difficult and sometimes delicate matter. My task, in exchange for what I like to think of as a fair retainer, is to recruit in absolute secrecy qualified personnel who can immediately step into the positions left vacant by these often abrupt changes in top-, middle-, and even lower-level management. Therefore, I wasn't at all surprised by the confidential nature of the union's approach. As I think I said, it happens quite frequently in my business."

"These people you recruited, were they for permanent or temporary jobs?"

Chanson thought about it for a moment. "I see no reason why I can't tell you that. They were all temporary jobs to last no more than six months."

"And when were you approached by the union?"

"A little over a month ago."

"How about being a little more specific?"

"In what way?"

"Was it after or before Arch Mix disappeared?"

"After."

"How long after?"

"As I recall it was two days after he disappeared. Possibly three, but no more than that."

"Did you connect the two?"

"The two what?"

"Mix's disappearance and the union's sudden demand for your services."

Chanson stared at me for several moments. "What I thought, Mr. Longmire, must, I'm afraid, remain confidential. However, I think it only fair to tell you that whatever my thoughts were, the FBI and the D.C. police were made aware of them the same day." He looked at his watch, a big, fat gold one that he kept in his vest pocket on a heavy chain. "I'm sorry," he said, "but I have another appointment."

"Just one more question," I said.

"Yes?"

"How did you turn up Ward Murfin for Roger Vullo?"

He picked up the grey file that he had placed on the table and leafed through it. When he found what he seemed to be searching for he looked back up at me.

"Murfin is an interesting type. I keep extensive files on such types because they are the kind of people who often are quite suddenly needed by the kind of clients that I sometimes serve. In fact, I think you'd be surprised at the files that I do keep. For instance, this one here." He tapped the folder on his lap. "It says in here that you really do keep bees, don't you?"

"Yes," I said. "I do."

21

Roger Vullo's office was only a short, hot walk from Jefferson Place, but I didn't notice the heat because I was too engrossed in putting the finishing touches to my theory about what had happened to Arch Mix and why. It was a sound theory, buttressed by solid facts with only a touch of wild surmise. I intended to lay it on Roger Vullo personally, collect the other half of my ten-thousand-dollar fee, and stop by a travel agent on my way home to make reservations for Dubrovnik. Two seconds after I entered Vullo's office I knew that I wouldn't be making the reservations just yet.

Vullo was savaging his right thumbnail as I walked in. He looked up and said, "You're late." Before he went back to his nail he used the hand he was working on to gesture at the other men in his office. "I think you know everybody," he said.

I thought so, too. One of the men was Warner B. Gallops. The other was my Uncle Slick.

Gallops grunted at me and Slick said, "I've been trying to get in touch with you, dear boy."

"I know," I said and sat down in a chair.

"There've been some extremely interesting new developments," Slick said. He reached over to Roger Vullo's desk and handed me the morning edition of the *Washington Post*. I looked at it, but saw nothing that was relevant.

"What page?" I said.

"The front page," Slick said. He nodded at Vullo and said, "I think you should play it for him first."

"Yes, it would probably save time," Vullo said. There was a small cassette tape recorder on Vullo's desk. He punched a button.

The tape whirred for a few moments and then a voice came on. The voice said, "This is Arch Mix."

There was silence on the tape for a second or two that was interrupted only by a slight crackling sound as if some paper were being unfolded.

The voice that was Arch Mix's went on: "To prove that this recording was made today I'm going to read you the top three headlines from this morning's edition of the *Post*."

I looked at the *Post* as the taped voice read the headlines. There was another pause, another crackle of paper, and then Mix's voice continued.

"I'm in good health and I've been reasonably well treated. My release depends upon your doing exactly what I tell you to do. It also depends on your making absolutely sure that you do not under any circumstances contact either the police or the FBI. I can't emphasize this too strongly. Do not contact the police or the FBI. If you do, I'll be killed. It's as simple as that."

There was another brief silence and then Mix's voice came on again. "The people who're holding me are serious. They mean business. They want two million dollars for my release. I repeat. Two million dollars. You're going to have to deliver it exactly when and where I tell you to. The money must be unmarked. It must be old or at least well used. Don't try anything tricky. If you do, you'll just get me killed."

Mix's voice, with its familiar deep rasp, was firm and authoritative until the last sentence when it cracked slightly. I didn't blame him. My voice would have cracked before then. There was another pause, another noise like the rustle of paper, and when Mix's voice resumed it sounded as if he were reading.

"What you've got to do is simple. After you get the

money, put it in two suitcases. Rent a black Ford LTD sedan.
Put the two suitcases with the money in its trunk. Make sure
the trunk is locked. At four o'clock this afternoon park the
car in the parking lot of the Safeway store near Chevy Chase
Circle. Do not lock the car. Leave the keys on the floor
under the accelerator and put a plain piece of white paper
under the windshield wiper. Typing paper will do. Don't
waste time trying to see who drives off in the Ford. He
won't know anything. Follow these instructions exactly and
they'll let me go. If you don't, they'll kill me. They mean
business.''

The tape whirred on for a few moments until Vullo
reached over and pressed another button. There was a
silence for several seconds that I finally broke with, ''Well,
he's alive, isn't he?''

''As of this morning,'' Slick said.

''Or eleven-thirty last night when the *Post* came off the
presses,'' I said. ''Who'd they send the tape to?''

''Me,'' Gallops said. ''It was inside my paper when I
went out to get it this morning.''

''You talk to Mix's wife?'' I said.

''She was the first one I talked to,'' Gallops said. ''She
agrees with me. We do exactly what Arch wants. No cops.
No FBI. But that left me with a problem so that's why I got
in touch with him.''

''Who?'' I said.

''With me, dear boy,'' Slick said. ''The problem was, of
course, the money. It would be impossible for the union to
put its hands on that much cash without attracting the
attention of the FBI and probably the police. So I suggested
a possible solution. Mr. Vullo has agreed to supply the
money.''

I looked at Vullo. ''You're going to put it up?''

''The Foundation is going to lend it to the union,'' he
said.

I looked at my watch. It was two forty-five. ''You haven't
got much time to get to the bank.''

''Fortunately, we started quite a bit earlier this morning,''
Slick said. ''By ten o'clock Mr. Vullo was on the phone

making arrangements for the money to be flown in from New York and Philadelphia.''

"You used several banks, huh?" I said.

Vullo nodded and then gave his thumbnail another bite. "Seven. Three in New York. Three in Philadelphia. And one here. The last of the money arrived approximately an hour ago. It's being counted and put into the suitcases now.''

I thought about what I'd just heard and been told for a few moments, and then I said, "It looks as though you're all set.''

"Not quite,' Vullo said.

"What do you mean not quite?" I said.

"We need someone to deliver the money," Vullo said. "I'd prefer it to be one of my associates.''

"Me?"

"I would've preferred both you and Murfin," he said. "Unfortunately, Murfin's still out of town.''

"I don't think I want to be responsible for two million dollars," I said.

"You won't be solely responsible, Harvey," Slick said. "I plan to accompany you.''

"He's gonna look after my interests," Gallops said. "The moment that money leaves the building it's gonna be the union's money. I'd like to make sure that there's somebody beside you, Longmire, looking after it.''

"Well," I said, "I'm flattered, but I still think I'll have to decline.''

"Mr. Longmire," Vullo said.

"Yes.''

"I believe that you have so far received only one half of the fee that we agreed on.''

"That's right. Half.''

Vullo opened his desk drawer, took out a cheque and used the eraser end of a yellow pencil to push it across the desk to me. "The other half," he said.

"Providing I deliver the money, right?''

"Yes.''

I looked at the cheque, but didn't touch it. Then I looked at Vullo. "You don't want to miss the ending, do you?"

"If this is the ending," he said. "If it isn't, then I think the Foundation's first report will be of remarkable interest."

"What the hell's he talking about?" Gallops said.

"Conspiracy," I said.

"Fuck yes, there's been a conspiracy. Arch got kidnapped and whoever did it wants two million bucks to let him go. That's a hell of a big conspiracy."

"You're right," I said, "but I think that Mr. Vullo was counting on something a bit juicer."

Gallops looked at Slick. "Now what's he talking about?"

"I'm not quite sure myself," Slick said, "except that I think both Harvey and Mr. Vullo were anticipating other developments and ramifications."

I looked at Gallops. "There'll be a lot of both when they let Mix go and he finds out what you've been up to."

Gallops stared at me for several seconds. Finally he said, "I got a call last night. Late last night. From St. Louis. They tell me you and Murfin were out there sticking your noses into things."

I nodded. "It was interesting. Sort of."

"Lemme tell you something else interesting, Longmire. When Arch disappeared, I took over and ran things the way I thought they oughta be run. Now if Arch comes back and he don't like what I've done, well, that's gonna be between Arch and me, isn't it? Not between anybody else. Just Arch and me." He looked at Slick. "I don't think this is such a hot idea. I don't need their fuckin' money. We can raise it someplace else."

Slick made a placating gesture. "You should remember the time factor."

Gallops thought about that a moment and said, "Well, I still don't like it. I don't like people sticking their nose in where it don't belong."

"Mr. Gallops," Vullo said, "I have already agreed that the Foundation would supply the ransom money. I did this because I felt that if there were a larger conspiracy involving Mr. Mix's disappearance, his return and his own account of what had happened to him would clarify everything. However, if you feel that we're invading your privacy, I'll withdraw my offer to supply the ransom.''

''What you're really saying is that you wanta talk to Arch when they let him go. Is that right?''

''That's right,'' Vullo said.

Gallops shrugged. ''If that's all you want, I don't give a fuck if you talk to him for a month. It'll be up to Arch. If he wants to talk to you, fine. If he don't—what the hell, that's your problem.''

Slick came in smoothly. He looked at his watch and said, ''Now that we all understand each other I think Harvey and I had best be on our way.'' He rose and looked at me, as though waiting for me to join him.

''I think I'll pass,'' I said.

''Shit,'' Gallops said.

Roger Vullo stared at me, an expression of curiosity and interest in his face. ''May I ask why?''

''Sure,'' I said. ''I think somebody should call the cops or the FBI. Let them handle it.''

''You heard Arch,'' Gallops said. ''Call in the cops and he gets killed.''

''Kidnappers always say that,'' I said.

''And a lot of people get killed, too,'' Slick said.

''Mr. Longmire,'' Vullo said. ''We had an agreement that you would spend two weeks on the Mix thing and then give me your report. It would seem to me that the conclusion of your report now depends on whether Mr. Mix is released by his kidnapper. You're not being asked to rescue Mr. Mix. You're simply being asked to help deliver the ransom safely. In exchange for that service I'm prepared to pay you the rest of your fee.'' He reached over and tapped the cheque with his pencil.

I looked at the cheque. I looked at it for several moments. Then I picked it up and put it in my pocket. ''I still think somebody should call the cops,'' I said.

22

I didn't count the money. I didn't even look at it. I simply picked up one of the suitcases and put it in the trunk of the black Ford that was parked in the basement garage of Vullo's building. The suitcase was heavy. About forty pounds. Slick put the other one in the trunk and then slammed the lid shut.

"Will you drive?" he said.

"Sure."

There was a long red light at the corner of M and Connecticut. I used the time to roll a cigarette. I was just pushing the lighter in when the signal changed. I turned the corner, the lighter popped out, I lit my cigarette, and said, "I thought he was dead."

"Mix?"

"Yes."

"So did I, dear boy, until just a few hours ago."

"You told me there was a chance he might be alive. A tiny chance, I think you said. What happened, did you get a tip?"

"It was a little more than a tip," he said.

"Are you going to tell me about it or do you want me to beg?"

"It was a phone call. It was from a black woman—or a woman who was trying to sound black."

"What'd she say?"

"She wanted to know how much the union would pay to

195

find out what had happened to Arch Mix. Well, there's the one-hundred-thousand reward that the union's offering, but when I told her about it she said it wasn't enough.''

''How much did she want?''

''She said she wanted two hundred thousand. I told her that was a great deal of money and that I would have to check with the union first. She asked how long that would take. I said at least four or five hours. She said she wasn't talking about that. She was talking about how long it would take before she could get the money. I said at least twenty-four hours, possibly forty-eight. She said, and I'll try to quote her exactly now, 'He'd be dead by then.' Then she said she'd call me back and hung up. She never called back.''

''When was all this?''

Slick thought about it for a moment as though trying to pinpoint it exactly. ''It was midmorning of the day that we had the picnic in Dupont Circle. About ten thirty.''

''The same day that Sally Raines got killed.''

''Yes.''

''And this was the tiny chance you told me about that Mix might still be alive.''

''That's right.''

''You ever tell the cops about it?''

''Yesterday,'' Slick said. ''I told them yesterday.''

''What'd they say?''

''That it was probably a crank call. There've been a lot of them.''

''It's funny,'' I said.

''What?''

''That they'd mention the same amount of money.''

''Who?''

''The woman who called you and Max Quane. Max told his wife that he was about to pull off some deal that would net him two hundred thousand. Max was shacked up with Sally Raines. Just before he got killed Max called me, half petrified, and said he thought he knew what had happened to Mix. A woman called you and told you the same thing, except that she implied that Mix was still alive. She also talked about two hundred thousand dollars. But the woman never called back—possibly because she was Sally who got shot to death that same afternoon, but not before leaving half a word that everybody seems to think is a vital clue.''

"A what?" Slick said.

"A vital clue. It's what the police are always finding except that Ward Murfin found this one. It supported what I call Longmire's Yellow-Dog Contract Theory, which isn't much of a theory any more.''

"Perhaps you'd better tell me about your vital clue first, dear boy.''

"It was on a wadded-up piece of paper that was found in Sally's room just before she got killed. It was one word. Chad. I thought it meant Chaddi Jugo.''

"Ah!" Slick said.

"You remember Chaddi.''

"Indeed.''

"That was your show, wasn't it, Slick, dumping Chaddi?''

"I was merely on the periphery.''

"I thought you thought it up.''

"I was only in on the initial planning.''

"Which was why you got me to go work for Hundermark.''

"It was the start of a brand new career for you.''

"Sure. Well, anyway Arch Mix once mentioned to Audrey that he wasn't going to let them do what they did to Chaddi Jugo—or something like that. Audrey remembers telling Sally that so she probably told Max Quane. I thought Max—and possibly Sally—had figured out who killed Arch Mix and why.''

"That was the basis of your Yellow-Dog Theory?" Slick said.

"Yellow-Dog Contract Theory.''

"I thought those contracts were against the law.''

"If my theory proved correct, they'd rewrite the law. My theory was that Arch Mix had been killed so that the PEU could strike ten or twelve of the biggest cities in the nation and create such a voter backlash that the Republicans would be guaranteed another four-year lease on the White House.''

Slick thought it over. "I can't say I object to the outcome, but the means seem a bit gamey.''

"They might even take the House of Representatives."

"Another decided improvement."

"You always did have funny politics, Slick."

"Just soundly conservative. A few of us are, dear boy."

"Of course there's still a certain amount of validity to my theory."

"In what way?"

"If whoever kidnapped Arch Mix doesn't let him go, then those strikes are going to take place."

"Unless—" Slick seemed to lapse into thought without finishing his sentence.

"Unless what?" I said.

"Unless, dear boy, the strikes were all Arch Mix's idea in the first place."

*   *   *

We drove into the Safeway parking lot at five minutes until four and parked the Ford about halfway towards the rear of the building. I handed Slick the keys and he opened the glove compartment and took out a plain sheet of 8 ½ × 11–inch paper. He gave me back the keys and I put them underneath the accelerator.

We got out of the car and Slick put the white sheet of paper underneath the windshield wiper. He looked at me. "Well, shall we take a cab?"

"Let's wait a few minutes," I said.

"I don't think that would be wise, Harvey."

"Mix didn't say not to watch who picked up the car. He just said that we shouldn't waste our time because whoever picks it up won't know anything. I'm curious."

Slick looked around. "I still don't think it's wise, but if you insist, let's at least make ourselves a little less obvious."

"What do you suggest?" I said. "After all, you used to do this for a living."

"You have some curious ideas about my former calling."

"Romantic notions, really."

"I suggest that we go stand with those other people over there by the entrance."

Some housewives were standing with their loaded shopping carts near the entrance of the store waiting for their husbands to drive up and put the groceries into their cars. Slick and I moved over and joined them.

At one minute past four a Yellow Cab pulled up in the driveway to the parking lot and discharged its passenger. He paid off the driver and started walking down a row of cars, turning his head from side to side. A few moments later he spotted the black Ford. He opened the door and felt underneath the accelerator for the keys. Then he removed the sheet of white paper from underneath the windshield wiper. He didn't bother to unlock the trunk and open the suitcases and count the money. Instead, he got into the car, started the engine, backed it out, and drove right past us as he headed for the Connecticut Avenue exit.

When he had got out of the cab I had got a good look at him. He was dark brown, slimly built, about six feet tall, and all of eighteen years old.

"They picked him up off the street," Slick said.

"You think so?"

"They probably paid him his cab fare and twenty dollars to pick up the car. They've probably got somebody on him to see if he's being followed."

"Then what?"

"He'll probably stop and make a phone call—to another pay phone. They'll tell him where to go next. It could go on like that for quite a while until they're sure that there's no one on his tail."

"Clever," I said.

"Crude, really, but effective."

"I wonder what their next move will be?"

Slick shook his head. "I have the feeling that we've heard the last of them. They'll probably wait until late tonight before they release Mix."

"Unless they kill him first."

"That's right," Slick said. "Unless they kill him first."

23

They found Arch Mix at 8:05 the next morning floating face down in the Anacostia River just south of the Frederick Douglass bridge. He had been shot in the back of the head three times. His body was identified by his wife.

I got some of this from a news bulletin that came over the radio at 9:15. The details I got from Slick who called at 9:35.

"Have you told Audrey?" he said.

"She heard it when it came over the radio."

"How did she take it?"

"Not too badly. She didn't say anything for a while and then she said she was going for a walk. She's still gone. Where are you?"

"I'm down at police headquarters with Vullo and Gallops. That's one of the reasons I'm calling. We've told the police of your minimal involvement in the delivery of the ransom and they'd like a statement from you."

"Today?"

"I don't think that'll be necessary. You can come in tomorrow just as well."

"Okay. I'll do it tomorrow."

"The other reason I called, dear boy, is that I've been thinking about your remarkable theory. Mix's death gives it a certain amount of validity, doesn't it?"

"I don't know," I said. "I haven't really thought about it."

"Well, there are a few bits and pieces that I've gathered over the past few weeks that, when put together with your own information, result in a rather startling picture."

"What're you getting at, Slick?"

"What I'm saying, Harvey, is that if we put our heads together, we may be able to prove not only your theory, but also prove who engineered the kidnapping of Arch Mix."

I was silent for a moment. Then I said, "You want to come out here?"

"I think that would be best, don't you?"

"Probably."

"What time is lunch?"

"When you get here."

"I'll bring some wine."

"Do that," I said.

After I hung up I called the Vullo Foundation and asked for Ward Murfin. I reached Ginger, his secretary, who said that Murfin hadn't come in yet and that she wasn't sure when to expect him.

I found his home number in our address book and called that. It rang three times before Marjorie answered it. Marjorie wanted to talk about the death of Arch Mix, which she had just heard about. She had some interesting theories about it, most of them involving the Palestine Liberation Organization. After we ran through those, I asked if I could speak to Ward.

"He's not here," she said.

"Do you know where he is?"

"He drove in from Baltimore late last night. He didn't get here till around two. We didn't get to bed until around three and then he rushed out of here this morning after he got the call."

"What call?"

"I don't know what call. All I know is that it woke us up about seven and he was gone by seven fifteen. He rushed out of here without even shaving although I told him he'd better shave before we go to Max's funeral."

"What time's that?"

"Aren't you going?"

"No, I'm still too broken up."

"Bullshit."

"What time's the funeral, Marjorie?"

"At two."

"If Ward comes in, ask him to call me."

"You ought to go to Max's funeral."

"I'll think about it," I said and then said good-bye.

I found Ruth in her studio which was a big-windowed room on the north side of the house. Honest Tuan was serving as a model. My nephew and niece were at Ruth's side watching her with fascination. I went over to see what she was doing. She was using watercolours and it seemed that the beavers who lived upstream were going to Honest Tuan's birthday party. Ruth had the beavers all dressed up.

She put her brush in a jar of water and looked up at me. She had a smudge of blue paint on the side of her nose, but then she usually did although it wasn't always blue.

"Slick's coming for lunch."

"That's nice," she said. "I hope he likes peanut butter and jelly sandwiches."

"He's bringing some wine."

"A good claret would go nicely with peanut butter and jelly."

"So would Mogen David."

"Since it's Slick, perhaps I should make him an omelette."

"I like your beavers," I said.

She looked at the watercolour critically. "They are rather precious, aren't they?" She turned to Nelson and Elizabeth. "Why don't you tell your Uncle Harvey what we've decided. *En français*."

"You do it," Nelson said and nudged his sister.

Elizabeth smiled her silky smile. "We will be very good and not bother our dear mother for the rest of the day," she said in her rapid French. "And if we are good, our dear uncle will let us swing on the swing and later he will take us to visit the beavers."

"Oh, what fun," I said.

"I think Audrey could use some solitude today," Ruth said.

"Probably."

"What're your plans?"

"Well, I think I'll go out on the porch and put my feet up and watch the Christmas trees grow."

"When I'm through with this I might come out and help you."

* * *

I sat on the porch watching the Christmas trees grow and going over it all in my mind, everything from Murfin and Quane's first approach until the news bulletin about Arch Mix's death, and by the time that Slick arrived at 11:30 I had decided that there indeed had been a conspiracy and that I was fairly sure that I knew who had both designed and executed it.

Slick looked hot and worried when he climbed the steps to the porch and handed me the bottle of wine. He looked around as if expecting to see someone.

"Where's Audrey?" he said.

"She hasn't come back yet."

"Are Ruth and the children here?"

"Over there," I said and pointed to where they were feeding the ducks.

"I think I was followed," Slick said.

"From where?"

"From Washington."

"All the way?"

"I'm not sure, but I think so."

"Let's go see," I said.

Slick loosened his tie, but didn't take off his coat. The loosened tie was ample evidence that he was concerned. He followed me down the stairs and around the house. A quarter of a mile away, where the dirt lane turned in from the wood, a car had stopped. It was pulled over to the edge of the lane. A man was on top of the car, reaching up with something shiny.

"I think, dear boy, that he's cutting your telephone wires."

"I think you're right."

We turned and hurried around to the other side of the house. I called to Ruth. She must have heard the note of alarm in my voice because she took the children by the hand and almost ran over to us.

"What's wrong?" she said.

"I'm not sure yet, but I want you to take the kids and go over to Pasjk's. Go to the other side of the pond and up through the trees and down. If Pasjk's phone is working, call the sheriff. If it's not, have him run you into town and tell the sheriff to get out here right away."

"Can't you come?"

"I'm going to see if I can find Audrey first."

"Where're we going?" Nelson asked.

Ruth made herself smile at him. "*En français*. You promised."

"Okay," Nelson said and then he said, "Where are we going?" in French.

"We're going to see Mr. Pasjk for some cookies and lemonade and maybe a ride into town."

"You'd better go now," I said.

Ruth nodded and started off around the pond. She stopped, looked back, and said, "Harvey."

"Yes."

She shook her head and smiled nervously. "Nothing."

Slick and I watched them until they disappeared into the pines. Then Slick said, "I hate to be an alarmist, but do you keep a weapon in the house?"

"An M-1 carbine."

"I think you'd best get it."

"I think you're right."

Inside the house, I went to the living room closet and opened the door. I kept the carbine on two pegs at the rear of the closet, but it wasn't there.

"I was wrong," I told Slick. "I don't have a weapon."

"What happened to it?"

"I don't know."

We heard the car making its way over the bumps in the lane. It was going a little fast and its tyres were bouncing up and grinding themselves against the fender wells.

"I don't think I want to wait for them, do you?" I said.

"I have no desire to," Slick said.

"Let's try the pines."

We hurried down the steps of the porch and ran around the pond and up into the pines. They were thick enough so that we couldn't be seen from the house, but if we carefully pulled some branches down we could watch the car as it pulled up and stopped near the house, not quite a hundred feet away.

The car was a black four-door sedan, a Plymouth, I thought. Its front doors opened and two men got out. A third man got out of the rear of the car. The three men had guns in their hands. I recognized the first two men. One of them, sitting outside my sister's house, had told me that his name was Detective Knaster, but he had lied. The other man was dark and had caterpillar eyebrows and the last time I had seen him he had been bounding down some stairs after having cut Max Quane's throat.

I recognized the third man with a gun, too. The third man was Ward Murfin.

24

Murfin led the way towards the house. The two men followed behind him for about five paces and stopped. The blond man went into a crouch and raised his gun with both hands. I recognized the crouch although the last time I had seen the blond man go into it he had been wearing a ski mask. A red one. So had the man with the caterpillar eyebrows, although his ski mask had been a different colour. Blue, I remembered.

The blond man was taking careful aim just as he had when he had shot Sally Raines. I yelled it as loudly as I could. I yelled, "Murfin! Behind you!"

It may have been something that he had learned from Filthy Frankie in Pittsburgh because Murfin went down into a tumbling dive and then rolled and kept on rolling. The blond man fired at him, but missed.

Murfin fired twice as he rolled and the blond man staggered, dropped his gun, clutched at his stomach just above the belt, and then sank slowly and perhaps even carefully to his knees. He stayed there on his knees for a moment before he toppled over onto his left side.

The man with the caterpillar eyebrows snapped two shots at Murfin, but when he didn't hit anything he darted back behind the parked Plymouth. Murfin got quickly to his feet and ran around the corner of the house just as the man with the caterpillar eyebrows aimed carefully and fired again. I didn't think that he had hit Murfin, but I wasn't sure.

"That's not quite the way we had it planned, dear boy," Slick said.

I turned and looked at the gun that Slick held in his right hand. It was aimed at me. It looked like a Walther, the PPK model. I had won one just like it in a poker game a long time ago.

"Well," I said, "thanks for letting Ruth and the kids go."

"I'm sorry, Harvey," he said. "I really am."

"Sure."

"I think it would be better if we went up the mountain a bit."

"Okay."

"You first."

I started through the pines up the mountain. "Whose idea was it, Slick, yours or Gallops's? But that's a dumb question; it had to be yours, didn't it?"

"Mr. Gallops's imagination is somewhat limited."

"The two-million dollars ransom. Do you split it?"

"You don't really think I was in it for the money, do you, Harvey?"

"No. Not really. I suppose you were in it for the power."

"And a certain amount of quiet acclaim," Slick said.

"Is this far enough?" I said.

"A little farther."

"Who backed you, Slick?"

"Some old friends and acquaintances put up the seed money although I didn't, of course, tell them specifically what I was up to."

"What did you tell them?"

"I merely outlined to them the political consequences of what you've chosen to call your Yellow-Dog Contract Theory. They were fascinated. I spelled it out only in general terms, of course."

"Probably on the golf course, wasn't it?" I said. "It's where all those heavy plots are hatched."

"Yes, as a matter of fact, several of our conversations did take place on a golf course. It's such a convenient spot. I remember that it was on the sixteenth green of Burning Tree that we came up with the perfectly marvellous idea of how we could channel the money with no danger of it ever being traced.''

"How?" I said.

"Unfortunately, dear boy, we're not going to have time to go into that."

I saw the movement up ahead of me. One of the pine branches trembled a little and I thought I caught a flash of brown. I didn't think it was a deer. I kept on going up the side of the mountain.

We went another twenty or twenty-five feet before Slick said, "I think this is about as far as we'll go, Harvey."

"Maybe we should talk it over," I said, raising my voice just a little.

"I think we've talked enough."

I decided to talk some more anyhow. It might just keep me alive. "You made a couple of mistakes, you know. Minor ones."

"Really?"

"They came to me this morning," I said, edging my volume up another notch. "There was only one person who knew where both Max Quane and Sally Raines were just before they were killed."

"And I was that person, of course. How very clever of you, dear boy."

"Max Quane called me at your place and I said his address out loud so I could remember it. You caught it. Then when Sally called Audrey, well, Audrey called you to find out where I was and you must have got Sally's address out of her. You had your hired guns hurry over and kill both Max and Sally."

"Harvey?"

"What?" I said.

"You don't want to turn around, do you?"

"Now!" I yelled and threw myself down and to one side.

Thirty feet or so up the mountain Audrey stepped out from behind a pine. She was wearing a brown shirt and tan slacks. She also carried the missing M-1 carbine. It was pointed casually at Slick.

I glanced back at Slick. He looked at me and then at Audrey. Audrey seemed to be the only danger so he raised the Walther carefully, aiming it at her with both hands.

"Don't do it, Slick," she said. "Please."

Slick aimed carefully. At thirty feet he would miss if he didn't. His mouth worked a little. Audrey brought the carbine up to her shoulder in one smooth motion and shot Slick through the head just below the left eye. Then she shot him in the throat as he fell and when he was sprawled on the ground she put two more shots into his body right above the heart.

I rose and quickly went up to her and put my arms around her, pulling her close to me. She was trembling. "I—I can still shoot, can't I, Harvey?"

"Yes."

"Jack taught me." Jack was Jack Dunlap, her dead husband.

"I know. I was counting on it."

"Jack said I was a good shot. A damned good shot. He always said that."

The trembling had turned into uncontrollable, almost violent shaking so I held her closer and tried to soothe her with meaningless words. She buried her head in my shoulder and started to sob. I held her even closer and as I did I could feel a kind of gentle sexual arousement. Audrey must have felt something too, because between her sobs, she said, "I don't give a damn! I want you to hold me. We don't have to be ashamed of it, do we, of holding each other?"

"No," I said. "There's nothing to be ashamed of."

Finally, her sobs stopped and she moved away from me. I found my handkerchief and gave it to her. She blew her nose and then looked up at me. "I didn't want you to fuck me," she said. "I just wanted you to hold me, but it felt like that, didn't it."

"Something like that."

"What are we, rotten or just normal?"

"Just normal, I think."

She looked down the mountain to where Slick lay.

"Goddamn you, Slick, anyway. What was the matter with him?"

"I don't really know."

"I heard you talking and I could make some of it out and then when you raised your voice, I could hear all of it. I'm not sorry I killed him. I'm just sorry that he was the way he was.

"Audrey?"

"What?"

"Why'd you take the carbine?"

She looked down at where she had dropped it. "I had some crazy idea."

"About what?"

"That I'd come up here on the mountain and pop a few pills and then put the muzzle in my mouth and pull the trigger. But I couldn't do it. Or maybe I just didn't really want to."

I knelt down and picked up the carbine and handed it to her. "Stay here until I come get you."

"Where're you going?"

"There's another one still loose down there near the house."

"What're you going to do, throw rocks at him?"

"I'll take Slick's gun."

I moved down to where Slick lay and picked up his gun. I looked back up at Audrey. She was staring at Slick.

"What do they call it?" she said.

"What?"

"Killing your uncle. It's not patricide or fratricide. It must have some Latin name."

"Avunculicide," I said, although I really wasn't sure.

I used the pines as cover to move south of the pond away from the parked Plymouth. I jumped across the narrow stream just below where the beavers were remodelling their dam and moved back into the pines again and started working my way down towards the house.

The trees thinned out fifteen or twenty feet from where the Plymouth was parked. I peered through the branches and saw the man with the bushy caterpillar eyebrows as he crouched by the car's rear fender, trying to look around it at the house. I couldn't see Murfin.

I took a deep breath, raised the Walther, and called, "Don't move!"

The man with the eyebrows moved anyway. He whirled around, searching for somebody to shoot at. I didn't know whether he could see me or not so I shot him in the left leg although I was aiming at his chest. He went down on his knees, but brought the gun up again and fired twice. I shot him again, this time in the shoulder, the left one, and when he still didn't go down, but once more brought his gun up, I fired again and this time the bullet hit him in the face just below his nose. The gun dropped from his hand and he pitched forward on to his face. He twitched once or twice and then after that he didn't move any more.

I left the trees and moved over to the sprawled man. He looked dead, but I couldn't bring myself to touch him to see whether he really was. Instead I walked around the Plymouth and called to Murfin.

He came slowly around the corner of the house, his pistol still in his hand. He looked at the blond man he had shot and then he looked at me.

"Where's the other one?"

"He's over there. Dead, I think."

"You shoot him?"

"Yes."

"Before that, I heard some other shots."

"That was my sister."

"Jesus. What was she shooting at?"

"My uncle. He's dead, too."

"They called me this morning," Murfin said. "They called me and when I got down there they gave me this story about you."

"What story?"

"About you and your uncle. They said that you and your uncle had Mix kidnapped. It was quite a story."

"Did you believe it?"

"Part of it. So I went home and got my gun and came out here with them."

"Just like that?"

"Lemme show you something," Murfin said. "Lemme show you who fed me the story and then maybe you'll understand why I came."

He went over to the Plymouth. "I wantcha to see this," he said. He opened the rear door. Lying on the back seat on his side with his knees drawn up to his chest and his thumb in his mouth was Roger Vullo. His eyes were open and staring. When I went closer I could smell the urine. Roger Vullo had wet his pants.

"Hey, Vullo," Murfin said.

Vullo didn't move. His eyes blinked once, but I don't think he really heard anything.

We stared at him for a moment and then Murfin slammed the rear door shut. "Well, at least he's not biting his fingernails any more."

"They're going to have to get some auditors," I said.

"For the Foundation?"

I nodded. "My uncle said that they'd thought up a way to channel the money. They used the Foundation. He and Vullo must have set it up that way."

"It was phoney, wasn't it? I've figured that out," Murfin said. "The whole fuckin' thing was phoney, right from the start."

"Right from the start," I said.

Murfin thought about it for a moment and then he looked at me and smiled one of those terrible smiles of his that almost made me want to turn away. "You know something?"

"What?"

"It damned near worked. Shit, I bet if they'd come to me, I could've figured out how to've made it work."

We heard the sirens then. It sounded as if they were drawing near, so we stood there and waited and listened to the sirens. When the sheriff's car turned into the lane I could tell that they were going far too fast. But The Proper Villain slowed them down. He always did.

25

It was the first Saturday in September and Senator Corsing and I were sitting on my porch, drinking gin and watching the sweet-voiced Jenny as she grasped the rope of the swing.

She looked back. "Like this?" she said.

"Like that," the Senator said.

She pushed off the rail of the porch and sailed out over the pond and when she let go she screamed just a little as she fell and her yellow bikini seemed to flash in the hot afternoon sun. She came up spouting and laughing and swam over to where Ruth was lying on the new raft that I had built.

The Senator took a swallow of his iced gin. "They held a meeting," he said.

"Who?"

"The candidates."

"Both of them?"

"Uh-huh. I put it together."

"What'd they meet about?"

"How to cover it up."

"Everything?"

"Almost everything."

"I didn't think anybody was going to do that anymore."

"Are you trying to be funny?"

"Just a little," I said.

"One of the problems was the money that your uncle raised."

"What about it?"

"They've managed to trace some of it. Where it came from. It went to the Foundation, of course, and then some of it went to the union. It helped pay the salaries of those two hundred guys they sent out. It's a real mess. If they disclosed where the money came from, then they'd have to tell where it wound up, so they decided that it was a no-win deal. Neither of the candidates would have an advantage and that's why they decided to put the lid on it."

"I suppose it makes sense."

"It does to a politician."

"Where'd the money come from?"

The Senator looked at me. "Where does big money always come from?" He took another swallow of his drink. "Your uncle had a lot of big-shot friends."

"Eight hundred," I said.

"Did he count them?"

"That's how many Christmas cards he sent out."

"He got to Vullo."

"Slick?"

"Yes. He got to Vullo with the idea of the Foundation. I don't know whether he knew Vullo was a little nuts or not. Anyway, it wasn't a bad idea. All that big corporate money going into a foundation that supposedly was set up to find out who really shot Jack Kennedy, et al. It was really rather clever, if you like that sort of thing."

"It sounds like Slick," I said. "He must have been the one who had Vullo bring me into it."

"Why?"

"Why was I brought in?"

"Yes."

"To poke holes, I guess."

"So that they could cover them up, if need be."

"Yes."

"Well, you did poke a few, didn't you?" the Senator said.

"And they almost covered them up, too."

"Yes," he said, "they did." He took another swallow of his drink. "It was really quite a scheme, wasn't it? First, they set up the Foundation. Then your uncle and Vullo had Mix kidnapped. After that they went to Gallops."

"What'd they offer him?"

"The two million in ransom. That was the carrot. The stick was that if he didn't go along with the strikes, the same thing could happen to him that happened to Mix. Or worse. He believed them. I'm not sure that I blame him."

"You think they'll ever find him?"

"Gallops?"

I nodded.

"I'm not even sure that they're looking for him too hard. The Candidate told me that they've heard rumours that he's somewhere down in the Caribbean. Spending the money, I guess. It should take him a while to spend two million."

"What's the diagnosis on Vullo?"

The Senator shrugged. "They've got him in this sanitarium in upstate New York. He's catatonic—just like my wife. Did I tell you I'm going to divorce her?"

I shook my head.

"I filed for it two days ago when I was back in St. Louis. If the voters don't like it, fuck 'em. I can always open a diner. While I was out there I also saw Freddie Koontz. He got his old job back."

"That's good," I said.

"He told me about you and Murfin at that meeting. Does Murfin always carry a blackjack?"

"I don't know."

"Well, the Candidate put him on the payroll as you suggested so maybe somebody should tell him to leave the blackjack home."

"Why?" I said. "The campaign's still got two months to go. Maybe it'll come in handy."

"You may be right," he said. "The Candidate also asked me to find out what you want. I told him I'd ask."

I took a swallow of my gin and got up. "I don't want anything," I said.

"Nothing at all?"

"Not anything that anybody can give me," I said and used the bamboo pole to pull the swing in. The Senator put down his drink and stood up, remembering to suck in his stomach so that it wouldn't bulge out over his trunks. He climbed up on to the porch rail, grasped the rope, and pushed off. As I watched the Senator fall, I wondered what the weather would be like in Dubrovnik.